SOUTHERN COMFORT

A Book in the Honkytonk Angels series

By Ciana Stone

Chapter One

Lengthening shadows slanted across the yard like fingers seeking purchase. Riley rocked back in his chair on the porch and took a sip from his coffee mug. It'd been a long day but a good one. He and his crew finished the new fence in the eastern pasture, a job that had taken the better part of two weeks. Riley was glad to have it done, but would likely be feeling it in his back for a week.

He grimaced as he shifted in the wooden chair to prop his booted feet on the carved log that served as a footstool. It was nice to have a little peace and quiet. Particularly after today. One of his new hands, Bobby Daniels, a twenty-two-year-old kid from Dallas, had never worked a ranch before and had to be taught everything. The boy was full of energy and never stopped asking questions. He'd helped out on the fence today and Riley was convinced that if he possessed half the energy Bobby used for talking, he'd be less than half as tired right now.

Not that Riley really minded. Bobby was a good kid and eager to learn. It reminded Riley of his youth and the things he learned from his dad. That brought a ghost of a smile to his face. His father had been gone nearly twenty years, but rarely a week went by that Riley wasn't reminded of him.

It had only been that way since he returned to Cotton Creek. Was it being back on the family land that prompted the memories? If it was, it didn't matter. He was content the way things stood. He liked thinking back on the things he'd learned from his father.

Dust appearing on the road leading to the ranch drew his attention. A minute or so later, an old truck pulled up his driveway. This time the smile that appeared on Riley's face was full blown. Billy Sweet climbed out of the truck with a paper bag in one hand and his cane in the other.

Riley couldn't remember a time he didn't know Billy Sweet. The Sweets, like his people, the Morgan's, had been in Cotton Creek for generations. Billy was a bit older than Riley but they'd been friends since Riley was knee-high to a grasshopper.

Now in his mid-fifties, Billy walked with a limp from an injury he earned helping a woman and her child from an overturned truck eight years back. His tall frame carried more weight than he'd sported in his youth and while his hair was liberally dusted with silver, his eyes were still clear and bright and his smile as infectious as ever.

Riley stood as Billy walked over to the front steps.

"Evening, Billy. What brings you out this way?"

"Stella Mae cooked this up fresh and said I should come on over and bring you some."

"Is that apple fritters I smell?"

"Best in Cotton Creek."

"Well take a load off and let me get you some coffee."

"Sounds good."

As Billy settled his stocky frame into a rocker, Riley went into the house, poured another cup of coffee and returned to the front porch.

"You not working tonight?"

Billy glanced up and accepted the cup of coffee. "Thanks. Naw, took the night. The Missus wants me to start letting the girls close up. Spend more evenings with her."

"Then what're you doin' on my porch, Billy?"

"Stella Mae's at her book circle or whatever it's called. Said for me to bring over these fritters and be home by nine sharp."

"Well, then I guess you've got time to help me polish off these fritters." Riley claimed his seat and reached for the bag sitting between their chairs. He pulled out a fritter and passed the bag to Billy. After settling back in his seat, he took a bite and groaned appreciatively.

"Never tasted anything as good as Stella's fritters."

Billy mumbled agreement around a big bite of pastry, chewed and swallowed. "Hannah says that young buck you got working for you can't talk 'bout nothing but what he's learning here."

"Oh?"

"He found his way to the bar 'for he'd been here a week, and now shows up every few days for a plate of pork and a few beers. Boy can't keep his trap closed two red-hot seconds."

Riley wasn't surprised that Bobby had found his way to Billy's Bar and Barbecue. Not only was it the only bar in Cotton Creek, but the barbecue Billy cooked up every weekend was the best in three counties.

Nor was he shocked that Bobby would find a willing ear in Hannah Sweet. Billy's middle child, Hannah, was as sweet as the day is long. She favored her mother, blond, with peachy skin, bright eyes and a figure that would've made him another eager buck vying for her attention, if he was twenty years younger.

Riley chuckled. "Yeah, he asks a blue million questions. Today it was about roping."

"Getting roped or slinging one?"

"I'm guessing the latter. That reminds me, Cody left her gear here the other day. Want me to get it and load it into your truck?"

"Naw. She'll be by when she wants it."

"That girl's something. She's gotta whole lotta you in her, Wild Bill." Back in the day, Billy Sweet had quite a bit of wild in his blood. It was Stella Mae who'd settled him down, and probably saved him from himself.

Billy laughed. "Don't she just?" He sobered. "I tend to worry some about her."

"Some people don't take hurt well, Billy. When she's ready to let it go, she will."

"It's been three years since that boy done her wrong. And not once has she ever mentioned his name."

"He broke her heart."

Billy turned his head toward Riley. "She talked to you about it, didn't she?"

"Not much."

"You'd tell if she was in a bad way, wouldn't you?"

It wasn't hard to see the concern on Billy's face. Riley knew that Billy would do anything for his family and when one of them was hurting, it worried him a lot. "You know I would. She'll be okay, Billy. You know your daughter. Cody doesn't give her heart easy and if someone steps on it, well, it's gonna take her a while to trust anyone with it again. But she will. Just let her do it in her own way."

"Don't see as I have much choice. And speaking of Cody, I'm supposed to ask you if you're headed to the bar this weekend. Fred, Jimmy and Otis said something about playing and she said it's time you dragged your tired old ass in and made some music.."

"She did, did she? Well then I reckon I better. When?"

"Saturday? Putting a good- size pig on Friday night so there's liable to be a crowd."

"Yeah, I'll be there."

A 'ping' noise had Billy looking in Riley's direction. "That you?"

Riley fished his phone out of his shirt pocket, looked at it and then laid it on the porch rail.

"Anything important?"

"Naw, just a friend."

The phone pinged again but Riley ignored it. He hadn't told Billy about Analise and he didn't know that he would. This seemed like a good time to change the subject.

"I hear you've been talking to those windmill folks."

Billy grunted and shifted to pluck another fritter from the bag. "Yeah. Cody's doing a fine job on the ranch, but it ain't making a lot of money. And we – Stella Mae and me – we're okay but we've been talking about slowing down a bit."

"And how does leasing your daddy's land for a windmill farm tie in with that?"

"Good old US greenbacks, buddy. There's a tidy sum involved. Good yearly income. With what they're willing to give, we could pay off the house in town."

"Okay, but again where does the slowing down part come in?"

Riley's phone pinged again. Billy gave it a sideways glance and took a bite of fritter. When Riley didn't touch the phone, he responded. "I been thinking of giving the bar to the girls. Hannah spends as much time there as she does at her mama's bakery, and Cody – well if she didn't have the bar she'd just be sittin' out there at the ranch by herself all the durn time."

"You'd walk away from the bar?"

"Well, no. I'd still be around. I just think it's time to give my girls a stake in something."

"And spend more time with Stella?"

"Yep."

"Doing what?"

"Dang if I know."

Riley's phone gave another ping and Billy gave it another look. "Sounds like that friend again."

Riley polished off the last of his fritter and washed it down with coffee. He knew that look in Billy's eye. Like a dog worrying a bone, the questions would keep coming and truth be told, he didn't know why he was keeping it a secret. It wasn't like he was having sexting with some woman or thinking he was in love. "All right, it's like this. About a year ago I – I went on Facebook."

"That computer thing where people tweep?"

"Tweet. And no, that's something else. Anyway, this lady, Ana Lise, who writes romance books, sent me a message asking questions about ranching. I answered and over time we got to be friends."

"So what does ranching have to do with romance books?"

"Apparently she writes about ranchers and cowboys."

"That right? She live round about these parts?"

"No. New York City. Manhattan."

Billy burst out laughing. "A New York woman writing about ranching? Kinda like Eskimos writing about surfing, ain't it? I sure hope she's asking the right questions."

"Well, she asks a lot of them."

"So you taken with this gal?"

"Billy, I haven't ever met her. We just send messages."

"Well, that being the case, now might be a good time for me to mention that Stella Mae said that Clara Jean Tilton's sister – you know, the widow woman? Anyways, she's thinking right strong about moving back to Cotton Creek. And according to Clara, she's quite a looker and –"

"No. No, and oh hell no. I appreciate Stella thinking of me but the last thing I need is a woman."

"Yeah, I told Stella Mae you'd say that."

"Well thank you."

"Course that don't mean I believe it. Now don't go giving me the stink eye. Them fancy women you took up with in Hollyweird might not a been worth a plug nickel, but having a good woman…well, there ain't nothing better in life, Riley."

"I wouldn't dispute that. But some of the fault was mine, Billy. I wasn't any better a husband than they were wives. Maybe I'm just not cut out for it."

Billy nodded and stared out at the growing darkness. "You ever miss it?"

"Being married?"

"No, Hollyweird."

That was a question Riley had asked himself nearly every week since he'd been back in Cotton Creek. "I did. Well, not at first. At first I was just glad to be away from it. But after about a year I started to miss it some – wondered what it would be like if I went back.

"Then..." he paused and looked at Billy. "Then you got hurt saving that woman and child when they went off the bridge and into the river, and your daddy got killed. Cody came ripping back home, all piss and vinegar, ready to load up the double barrel and go to war. Once she found out there was nobody to shoot, she got all hell bent on being here and taking care of everything. Your mama was a wreck and Stella was a mess, all torn up. Poor little Hannah had her hands full trying to take care of her mama, keep Cody from going off the rails and give little KC some attention."

Billy nodded, and swiped at the corner of one eye. "I didn't know what they were going through."

"Course not. You were unconscious for a week and your girls were all scared to death you weren't gonna wake up."

"I 'preciate all you did for them Riley. I shoulda found a way to thank—"

"Don't you even say it Billy. We're friends. And I did it cause I wanted to. Your family took me in when I got back – made me feel like I was part of a family. I love all those girls like they were my own. But the point is, that made me realize that what I have here is real. Substantial."

"So you don't miss it. Hollyweird, I mean?"

"Not a bit."

"I'm glad to hear that. But let's get back to this New York gal. Your durn phone's done dinged a dozen times. I think you best get on that thing and answer that gal or she might not be inclined to be your friend much longer."

Riley smiled. "Maybe."

"And I gotta get. By the time I get home, Stella Mae will be coming home."

"You tell her I said thank you for the fritters."

"You know I will." Billy shoved himself up out of the chair. "And we'll be seeing you on Saturday?"

"You bet'cha. I'll stop by on Thursday if you want and help you get that pig in the smoking pit."

"That'd be a real help. I 'preciate it."

"My pleasure. Now get on before Stella gets mad at me for keeping you too long.""

Billy chuckled. "Yeah, I'm going. You have a good night, my friend."

"You too, Billy. Thanks for stopping by."

Riley watched Billy amble out to his truck, get in and drive away. He sat there for a few minutes, thinking about what he'd said to Billy. Speaking the words made him realize how much he meant them. He never expected to consider Cotton Creek home again, but that's just what it had become.

It might be a bit lonely at times, but nothing was perfect. His phone pinged and he pulled it from his pocket. Riley read the string of texts and burst out laughing.

Chapter Two

Analise was just coming in from taking her ruined clothes to the outside trash when her phone chimed. She rushed to get it from the charging stand on the kitchen counter.

It was Riley.

Not to laugh at your expense, but that did give me a chuckle. Mineral spirits should take that right off.

Analise smiled. Her online friend, Riley, was a woodworker as well as a rancher and musician. She'd found an unfinished chest online and wanted to finish it herself, to store mementos in, things that had no value other than sentimental.

She'd asked him for advice on how to do it, and had followed his instructions step-by-step. The only problem she had was that she'd started with two rags and somewhere along the way had ended up sitting on one that was soaked with stain.

Which meant that her thin cotton pants ended up stuck to her. The pants and her rear end were coated with a nice warm red chestnut stain. She'd managed to peel the pants off, but had stain in places that were never meant for it.

Analise had thrown on an old pair of her husband's sweat pants long enough to take the ruined clothes to the outside trash can. Thank god Riley had responded to her text or she'd have been thinking about soaking her butt in turpentine.

Thanks. She typed. *I was about to head for the turpentine. I did buy a big jug of mineral spirits, like you suggested. Good thing I didn't opt for the small size.*

So stained lady parts aside, how did the chest turn out?

She smiled. *Really good. Tomorrow I will put that tung oil stuff on it.*

Analise put her phone down and opened the refrigerator. She hadn't eaten all day and was suddenly starving. She looked at the phone on the counter when it chimed.

You might need more than one coat. Let it dry for a day before putting on the second one. And don't forget to buff it after the first coat.

She gave the contents of the refrigerator a glance, frowned and closed it. *I will. How'd your day go? Get that fence finished?*

Yes ma'am. Sure did.

Another smile crossed her face. Even in text, Riley sounded Texan. She wondered, not for the first time, what his voice would sound like. She might have already had that answer had they not agreed to keep the communication limited to messages.

Maybe it was better that way. She could imagine his voice to sound just as she wanted. Just as she could imagine him looking like her perfect fantasy image of a rancher. God, he'd never speak to her if he knew all of the fantasies she'd cooked up about him during the lonely nights. The smile faded as the house phone rang. She checked the caller ID. It was her husband. This couldn't be good.

Gotta clean up and fix dinner. Have a good night, Riley.

You too.

Analise leaned back against the kitchen counter. She could either return her husband's call or get clean.

Getting clean won.

It took four rags and a quarter of the bottle of mineral spirits to get all of the stain off, but she finally managed, showered and dressed in a pair of loose gauze cotton pants and an old, oversized t-shirt.

When she returned to the kitchen with the rags secured in a plastic bag, her husband, Rodrick Becke, stood at the center island, a bottle of Scotch on the island and a half-full glass beside it.

"What are you doing here?" She stopped cold, clutching the plastic bag.

"Where's my money?"

"Pardon?" She tried to cover her surprise and the little spike of fear that question generated. An idea occurred to her and she quickly went to the kitchen counter where her phone lay. After picking it up, she accessed the record function and then shoved the phone in the pocket of her pants.

"Don't play dumb. I know you cleaned out half the balance of the Seychelles account and the Belize account is also down fifty percent."

"Oh that." Analise had recovered from the surprise of seeing him standing in the kitchen. "I only took my half."

"Your half?" His shout had her wincing, a fact that annoyed her. She was sick and tired of being afraid, of being lied to, used and treated like a dimwit.

"Yes, my half."

"You don't have a fucking half."

"I do now." She marched around him and through the kitchen to the laundry room. From there, she stepped out into the garage and crammed the plastic bag into the large trash can.

When she turned back toward the house he was blocking the door. "I want my money, Analise."

"It's not your money, Rick."

"The fuck it's not."

"Get out of my way."

"Or what?"

The threatening tone of his voice gave her pause. Would Rick physically hurt her? He'd always been one to fly off the handle, shout, stomp around and even destroy things, but he'd never raised a hand to her.

"Get out of my way."

"Give me my money or you'll be sorry."

"Oh I'm already sorry. Sorry I didn't see what was going on under my nose the last five years. Sorry I didn't realize you and your whole family were a bunch of crooks. Sorry I wasted twenty-five years of my life with a man who has no regard for anyone other than himself. But you know what? I'm tired of being sorry and scared that I'm going to displease you by saying the wrong thing, wearing something you don't like or having friends you don't think meet your social standing. I'm tired of everything about my life and I'm keeping that damn money and starting a new one.

"One that doesn't include you."

"You walk and you'll never see your son again."

Analise pushed past him and returned to the kitchen. "Oh please. David is twenty-two years old and news flash, finished moving to Cambridge two days ago."

"You move and I'll stop payment on his tuition and his apartment."

"Go ahead. That money I took was put into an account in his name. An account you can't touch. His education is paid for and with what he'll have left when he graduates, he will be fine."

"That's my money!"

"Not anymore. Oh, and while we're at it, I transferred all of the money from our two savings accounts here along with the checking account into an account of my own. I figure that's a fair distribution. You take the house and whatever else we own and I take that."

"You fucking bitch."

"Call me what you want, but like I said, I only took half. Actually less than half. You've still got plenty in your offshore accounts, and if the allegations against you and your family's company are true, there's millions hidden somewhere – millions you stole from your clients. So, unless they throw your sorry ass in prison, you and your mistress should be able to live high on the hog In fact, you can do it here just as soon as I leave."

"Leave? Where the hell do you think you're going?"

15

"None of your damn business. Now get out. I'm finished talking to you."

"This isn't over."

"Oh yeah, it is."

"I'll burn this fucking house to the ground and you in it."

"Oh?" She turned to him with a smile, holding her phone. "Well, we'll see about that."

"What the fuck are you doing?"

She quickly messaged the recording to her attorney and also to her best girlfriend, Katie. "Making sure it's on record just in case anything unfortunate happens to me or this house."

Rick snatched up the glass from the center island and hurled it at her. Analise ducked and the glass smashed into a cabinet, shattering all over the counter top and floor. What the hell? He'd always had a short fuse but this was getting out of hand. And it was scaring her a little. Not that she was going to let him know that so she bolstered her courage and spoke slowly and with as much menace as she could muster.

"Get out or I'm calling the police."

He slung the bottle of Scotch at her and shouted. "You're a fucking bitch. I don't know why I didn't divorce you years ago."

That tore it. She'd ducked the bottle when it bounced off the cabinet door behind her, hit the counter with a crack and then exploded on the tile floor.

"I wish you had. Now get out!"

He gave her a glaring look " You might think you've won, but trust me, you haven't. I'll get even with you, you bitch. When you least expect it. You can take that to the fucking bank."

He then stomped out of the room, tossing one final snipe over his shoulder. "Fuck you."

"Not ever again." She muttered to his back.

A few seconds later she heard the front door slam. She hurried to it to insure it was locked and leaned back against it. She and Rick had been through a few arguments over the years, and while he wasn't above throwing a fit, stomping about and shouting, he'd never been this bad. Whatever was going on in his life, it must be really bad. That thought prompted her to do a quick Google search on her phone. Within seconds she'd found what she wanted and placed a call.

"Hi? Bob's Lock and Key? Is there any chance I could get you out here this evening to change the locks in my house? Someone stole a set of keys and I really would feel more secure if the locks were changed. Oh, okay, yes, I understand. That will be fine. Yes, see you soon."

She wasn't thrilled to pay twice the going rate to get the locks changed but she would feel better knowing that Rick couldn't get in if he decided to come back.

As she busied herself cleaning up the broken glass and liquor, she thought about what a mess her life had become. It was time to start over. David was settled in Cambridge and she'd discussed her plans with him.

He'd encouraged her to do what made her happy. They'd see one another during his breaks and at holidays. He thought it was past time for her to start living for herself instead of in his father's shadow.

17

Well, that's exactly what she was going to do. Tomorrow she had an appointment to look at a small RV. She had no idea where she wanted to live, but was quite certain it was far, far away from Rick. And she'd always wanted to travel around, see different parts of the country.

Maybe she'd even get an idea for a new book. Her last one had not broken any sales records, but she was finally starting to earn a decent amount each month from her writing. Who knows, maybe she'd even make it down to Texas and meet Riley in person.

Or not. One thing her life had taught her was that fantasy was almost always better than reality. Right now, Riley was a bit of a fantasy. He was kind and had a good sense of humor and she imagined him as a tall, lanky cowboy with that low center of gravity glide of a walk and a smile that would light up any room he entered.

Chances were, the real Riley would never measure up to her fantasy version.

Her phone rang and she hurried to check the caller ID. "Katie, hi. What's up?"

"OMG, girl why are you not on the phone with the police this very minute? I was going to call them myself if you didn't answer. What an asshole!"

"I'm taking that to mean you listened to the recording I sent you."

"Well, duh! Analise, you've got to get away from that man. I'm serious, honey."

"I know and I am. I promise."

"Okay, OMG, I just remembered! Girl, you *have* to come to San Antonio in September."

"I do? Why?"

"There's going to be a convention here. I'll send you the link. Lots of great writers and readers. It's only three days but sounds like it will be a blast."

"September? I don't know. I'll think about it. Depends on…well, you know."

"Yeah, I hear ya. When you think you'll be leaving?"

"Soon. I'm going to look at that RV in the morning."

"Analise, have you ever driven an RV?"

"No."

"And you do know how big they are, right?"

"Yes, but I told you, this one is small. You don't have to have a special license. Just perfect for one person."

"Yeah, and you really think you'll be happy out there on the road, all by yourself, staying in campgrounds?"

"I don't know. Maybe."

"No room service."

"I *can* cook, Katie."

"Yeah, so can I but it doesn't mean I like to. And I worry about you being on the road alone."

"I know and I appreciate that but I really want to do this. I need to do it. I've never been on my own, Katie and I want to – I don't know, I want to do something completely unconventional for once."

"Like come to Texas for the convention and see your bestie?"

Analise laughed. "Yeah, something exactly like that. Tell you what, send me the link and I'll check it out. Right now, I've got to find something to eat, I'm starving."

"Okay, hon. Will do. Call me after you see the RV."

"I will. Love you."

"Love you, too."

Analise ended the call and leaned back against the counter with a smile. Leave it to Katie to lift her spirits and present an opportunity. She could take her time on her trip and if she timed it right, she could stop in and spend a couple of days with Katie and then hit the convention.

Then, well maybe she'd think about asking Riley if he wanted to meet. It wasn't like she expected them to take a look at each other and fall madly in love, but despite reality not surpassing fantasy, he had become a really good friend and she'd like to meet him in person.

The doorbell rang and she remembered the locksmith. Hurrying to the door, she dismissed thoughts of Texas and focused on the right now – namely making sure Rodrick Becke didn't set foot in this house again without having to break the damn door down.

Chapter Three

Rodrick closed the lid on his laptop and swiveled in his chair to face the ceiling-to-floor bank of windows behind him. Fifty floors up, his office looked out over New York, sprawled like a decadent whore, a bit rough around some edges but still the most magnificent piece of ass in the brothel.

He'd always thought of New York as his, as if he commanded the city, sitting in his steel and glass tower, moving money across continents, affecting economies, controlling lives and industries. It made him the next thing to a god, and he was addicted to the power it bestowed.

He sighed and stood, jamming his hands into the pockets of his pants. Things were starting to look serious. His father and brother had assured him that no one could prove Becke Ltd was guilty of any wrong-doing. He'd been given assurance that great care had been taken to make sure the family and the company were protected.

It was not what they said that bothered him, as much as what they did not say. His brother Rolf had brought business into the company that was tainted with the stench of organized crime. If it had been only of a domestic variety, it would have boded ill, but Rolf was an ambitious man. Becke Ltd was now in bed with criminal organizations around the globe.

Dirty money was laundered every day. Rolf often laughed that they were the world's most profitable cleaners. There was a time Rodrick had tried to laugh about it, but the truth was, he'd never wanted to be part of that. Sure, he wasn't above juggling the books to put more in his own pocket, but he was very careful to make sure what '*extra*' he took was taken in small, virtually unnoticeable amounts.

21

When billions of dollars were trading hands every year, funneling a half of a percent to an off-shore account was child's play. What Rolf had gotten them into could not only land them behind bars, but quite possibly six feet under. Rodrick was getting jumpier by the day, looking for threats at every turn.

With a groan he pulled his hands from his pockets and covered his face, his fingers massaging the orbits of his eyes where a stress headache threatened. Damn Analise. She'd wrecked everything. If she'd left things alone, he could have taken Gina and fled. But now that escape route had been ruined.

Damn Analise.

The sound of his office door closing had him whirling around with his heart pounding. He almost lunged for his desk drawer where he kept the handgun he purchased a few months ago. What met his eyes didn't slow his heart-rate, but the speed had nothing to do with fear. Gina Russo. Just looking at her aroused him. Even now he marveled that she had fallen for him.

Gina was not yet thirty, had the body of a Victoria's Secret model, a face beautiful enough to stop traffic and was, without a doubt, the most passionate, and inventive lover imaginable. There was nothing she wouldn't try and she indulged his every fantasy.

Just looking at her inspired an erection. Rodrick had never wanted a woman the way he wanted Gina. She had appeared in his life during a time when he and Analise were little more than room-mates, navigating the house in ways to avoid running into one another.

Gina had brought laughter, excitement and passion back into his life. He would do anything to keep her.

"Gina, what are you doing here, darling?"

"I was worried." She crossed the room to him, her walk that sensual sway that made a man's eyes move up and down her body. "You were so distracted today at lunch and after that fight you had with—"

He put his fingers to her lips. "Shhh, I told you, it will be fine."

She raised both hands to wrap around his wrist and guide his finger into her perfectly colored and glossed lips. He couldn't stop the reaction of his body to her actions.

When she slid his fingers from her mouth, she dropped his hand and placed hers on his chest, leaning in a bit closer.."I'm frightened, Ricky."

"Of what?"

"My safety. My credit card. The one you got me a few months ago. It was declined today at Macy's. And when I left, two men in a dark sedan followed me at Macy's, and when I left I was followed by two men in a dark sedan)

"Are you certain they were following you?"

"Yes. They pulled up to the curb when the driver stopped at the penthouse."

Rodrick pulled her into his arms. "I'll figure a way out of this, Gina."

She pushed back to look at him. "You better."

With that she pulled away, hugging herself. "I wake at night in a cold sweat, imagining what kind of financial ruin this could put you in."

She pivoted on one sharp pointed stiletto to face him. "Are you sure you don't know where the money is?"

"Yes, I told you. I've looked but Rolf has me locked out of some parts of the system and—"

"Then find someone who can let you back in! Ricky, you have to do something!"

"I know. And I'm trying. I swear I am. Just give me a little more—"

"No." Gina held up one manicured hand. "I love you, Ricky, but I live in a state of anxiety and I can't go on like this. You have to do it now or…or I will have to – to walk away."

"No!" He rushed to her, taking her by the arms. "No. You can't leave me."

"I can. I won't have a choice if you don't do something."

I'll fix this Gina. Somehow I'll fix it. I promise. I'll find enough to satisfy them for now until I can figure out where the rest of it is."

"What about the money your wife stole from you? Can't you get that?"

"She put it in an account in her name only."

"But you're her husband."

"That doesn't matter. Unless she dies, I can't touch it."

"So you can't touch it even though you're married but if she died you could? That doesn't make sense."

"It's because of our wills. Were she to die, her will gives me everything she has, including the money she took."

"Then it's a shame that bitch didn't get run over by a truck today."

"Gina, darling, you don't mean that."

"Oh yes I do. It's her or us, Ricky. Which is more important to you?"

Rodrick pulled Gina into his arms to hide his expression from her. She'd always been able to read him and he had no desire for her to know the chill her words gave. He'd admit that he was furious with Analise for taking the money, but even so, he wouldn't wish death on her. He might have stopped loving her a long time ago, but he didn't have the heart to wish for something like that.

Still, that horrible little voice inside his head said that it would make things a lot easier. If he had that money, he could pacify the people who posed the greatest threat to him. Or he'd have enough to run away with Gina and live comfortably for the rest of his life.

If only he had that money.

*****

Distant lightning drew Riley's attention as he stepped out of his truck in the parking lot of Billy's Bar. The weather forecaster had damn near crowed with the announcement they had a sixty percent chance of rain tonight. Riley would believe it when he saw it. The drought of the last few months was hurting everyone, ranchers and farmers alike.

Were it not for Cotton Creek, which ran right smack dab through his property, he'd probably have lost a lot of his herd. Now the creek was running lower than it had in the last decade. Hoping that distant lightning was the portend of a house- shaking, gully-washer of a storm, he reached inside his truck for his guitar case.

25

A dozen or more voices called out greetings the moment he walked into the bar. Riley couldn't help but grin. Billy's was the real life equivalent of *Cheers*. Here everyone *did* know your name. He returned the greetings as he walked over and took a seat on a stool at the end of the bar.

"What'cha having, Riley?" Cody Sweet, the tiny brunette woman behind the bar grinned at him.

"Whatever's on draft."

"It's on the house since you're playing."

"Well, in that case…whatever's on draft."

Cody chuckled and drew him a beer. "Dad tell you I have my eyes on a new mare?"

"Don't believe he did."

"She's a beaut. I'd like to breed her to Twostep."

"I thought your daddy said you were gonna get rid of that hellfire."

"He wants me to, but you know I love that horse. And he's only mean to people he doesn't like."

Riley chuckled. "Which is damn near everyone."

Cody grinned. "That new fella of yours has me teaching him to rope. Seems he has a hankering to try his hand at rodeoing."

"Yeah, he has a hankering to try his hand at everything."

"He is mighty enthusiastic."

"So how long's he been at it?"

"A couple of weeks. He's actually got potential. But I wanna pit him up against a feisty beast and I know you got that one cow that's ornery as a snake, so I was hoping I could ride over Sunday afternoon and round her up. If that's okay with you."

"Just fine. You wanna stay to dinner?"

"Are you cooking?"

This time it was a full-blown laugh that emerged. "Oh no. You, Cody Sweet did *not* cast aspersions on my skills in the kitchen. Why, if memory serves, the last time I was at your house for dinner-"

Cody tossed a bar cloth at him. "Don't say it."

Riley caught the cloth and grinned at her. "Yeah, I'm cooking. Steak and potatoes. Even I can't mess that up."

She laughed and snatched back the bar cloth. "Well fine then. I'd love to, Riley."

They and everyone else in Cotton Creek knew that there was a lot of things Cody Sweet could do, but cooking was not on the list. Unlike her mama and her sister, Hannah, Cody had no talent for cooking. In fact, Billy, her father, always joked that Cody could burn water.

"So." She leaned over the bar toward him. "What do you hear from Miss Stained Butt?"

"I should'a never told you that."

"Oh come on, it was funny. And it's not like I'm gonna tell anyone. But no matter what you say, Riley, I know there's something going on there. You been messaging with her for forever."

"Forever?"

"Well for a year at least. Come on, fess up."

"I told you, we're just friends."

"Yeah right. You ought to invite her to come down for the annual rodeo and barbecue bash. It's just around the corner. She might get a kick out of it seeing as how she writes those romance books about cowboys. And oh damn, I almost forgot. I read her last book and god as my witness, every time her hero, Colt, opened his mouth it was you."

"Excuse me?"

"He talked just like you."

"Along with half of Texas."

"No, it was you, Riley. I bet you a dollar to a donut she used you as her hero. I think she has a crush on you."

"She's never even met me."

"But you Facebook message with her more than KC Snapchats with her friends. Which reminds me, are you ever gonna put your picture on your profile?"

"Probably not."

"Well why not. Hell, Riley, you're hot – for an old guy, I mean."

"An old guy?" He pretended shock at the comment, knowing full well it was not intended as an insult.

"Well you are old enough to be my daddy."

"That I am."

"And if I didn't love you like family, I might even be tempted, so why not add a photo? I'll take one for you."

"You know why I don't."

Cody shrugged. "Sometimes you have to let go of the past, Riley."

"Hello pot. I'm Kettle, nice to meet you."

Cody's eyes narrowed for a moment but then she shrugged. "Yep, it takes one to know one, don't it? You want a refill on that beer?"

"You got any barbecue left? I didn't have time to eat."

"I made up some sandwiches for dinner. Wanna split with me?"

"How many you got?"

"Four."

"Well, if you're sure you can survive with just two."

"For you, I'll make the sacrifice. Let me run back and warm 'em up. Cole slaw and potato salad? Hannah made 'em both fresh today."

"That'd be good."

"You got it." She refilled his beer and then headed for the kitchen, hollering for her sister. "Hannah, watch the bar!"

Riley grinned and turned to look around. The place was pretty packed, but then it was almost nine o'clock on a Saturday night. Lot of folks looked forward to throwing back a few brews at Billy's. It was a place to socialize, dance and unwind from the week.

He spotted Otis, Jimmy and Fred on the old stage, setting up. Billy walked up behind him. "So you playing or drinking?"

"Little of both. Cody's gonna share her dinner with me. Didn't have time to eat."

29

"Cody's giving you half her food? Now that's love. Dang if she can't out eat half the men in Cotton Creek. Her mama spent half her childhood fearing she had a tapeworm."

"She can put it away."

"That she can. Okay, when you'd done, let's get to it."

"Yes sir."

Just as Billy was walking away, Riley's phone pinged in his shirt pocket. He pulled it out and read the message.

Well, it took me a longer than I thought it would but I made it to New Orleans and guess what I just did? I bought a voodoo doll! It's really ugly but New Orleans is amazing. Have you ever been here? It's my first time. I'm on Bourbon Street and I'm stopping at every bar. Not drinking at every one just stopping for a look.

The message was followed by a shot of Bourbon Street. Riley smiled and typed in a response. *Yeah, been there a time or two. Quite a place. Good thing you're not having a drink at every bar or you'd never make it to the end of the street. Have fun. Getting ready to play some at Billy's.*

There was only a few seconds' delay before her response came in. *Sure would like to hear you play one day, Riley.*

You should come to the annual Cotton Creek barbecue cook-off in October. Third weekend, starts on Friday and goes through Sunday.

Riley responded and hit the send key, then looked at it in horror. Why the heck had he done that?

This time the response was not instant. In fact, it took so long Riley started to think that not only was Cody wrong, she was miles off base about Analise having a crush on him. Had he just scared her?

When his phone pinged, he was both relieved and anxious.

I just might. I'm going to a writer's conference the second weekend of September in San Antonio then visiting a friend in the area. Will let you know.

Riley stared at the phone for a moment, trying to decide if he was happy or wished he'd never asked. It wasn't that he didn't want to meet her. They were pretty good friends, and truth be told, he looked forward to their messaging conversations more than he'd admit.

But he wasn't sure he was ready for a face-to-face. First of all, what if she recognized him? Would that change things? And second, what if – God forgive him – but what if she was just downright butt ugly?

That thought shamed him on a couple of levels. It shouldn't matter what she looked like, and besides, who said she was gonna show up looking for anything other than what they had. A friendship.

Damn if he wasn't letting Cody mess up his head with her talk.

"Someone piss in your beer?" Cody slapped two plates on the bar.

"Nope." He cut his eyes at her.

She shrugged and picked up one of the thick barbecue sandwiches from her plate to take a giant bite.

Riley shook his head and grinned. Cody might be pint-sized but her appetite was bigger than most men he knew. He'd never known anyone who could put away as much food as she did and remain a petite little thing with enough energy for five people. Maybe that's why it took so much to fill her up. She was a full eight-cylinder machine, running wide open all the time.

He took his time and finished one sandwich, the potato salad and part of the coleslaw. She'd polished off her entire plate of food before he reached for his near-empty beer mug.

"Refill?"

"No, thanks. Think I better mosey on over to the boys. They look a bit itchy to get started. Thanks for the dinner. I'll make it up to you on Sunday."

"Steak. Big one." She held her hands out wide enough to encompass a beach ball. "Just shy of mooing."

"You got it half-pint."

He picked up his guitar and headed over to the stage. Billy and Otis were on old worn stools, softly picking on their instruments – Billy on the banjo and Otis on the bass guitar. Fred was putting a new string on his old guitar and Jimmy was sitting behind his drums, tapping his sticks together.

"You boys ready to play?"

They looked up and him and Billy grinned. "Born ready. Let's do it."

Riley grinned and walked up to the mic, tapped on it and upon hearing the loud tap through the speakers, leaned in to talk.

"Hey, folks. Mind if we play you a tune or two?"

SOUTHERN COMFORT

Cheers and yells had him chuckling. "Any requests?"

The cacophony that ensued prompted a chuckle and Billy sidled up beside him at the microphone. "How's about an oldie but a goodie? Ring of Fire?"

"The Man in Black it is." Riley struck the first chord and the others picked up. He was glad Cody had goaded him to come in tonight. Playing with the band always lifted his spirits and the energy from the crowd never failed to fill him with gratitude. He sometimes forgot to appreciate what it meant to be able to just be Riley and not have anyone expecting larger than life actions from him.

Here it was okay if he missed a chord, or hit a sour note. These people were family and they wanted nothing more than to have some music, tap their toes, dance or sing along.

An hour later Riley held up his hand to the clapping crowd. "We're a bit parched so we're gonna take a break and be back in a few."

He made his way through the crowd to the bar. Cody grinned as she pulled a draft and then slid it down the bar to him. Riley caught it and gave her a grin and a nod before lifting it to his lips.

"Riley Morgan, there you are!"

Riley turned at the sound of the voice to find Stella Sweet standing behind him. With her was the skinniest woman he'd ever seen in his entire life. It was like the phrase "sack of bones" coming to life. Riley's first thought was that the woman was terminally ill, because there was no way a person would choose to be that skinny. His

33

second was that he hoped Stella wasn't trying to fix him up. Again. Please got let it be anything but that.

"Stella, hey. How are you?"

"Any finer and I'd need a manager. Riley, I don't know if you remember Agnes June Jones? Oh, Howard now. Clara Jean Tilton's sister? They were a couple of years behind us in school. Anyway, she's visiting Clara Jean for a few weeks and is thinking of moving back to Cotton Creek."

"Well that's real nice. Nice to see you Ms. Howard."

"Nice to see you, Riley." Agnes June gave him a big toothy smile and actually batted her eyes at him. "I just couldn't believe it when I first saw you on the big screen. To think that little Riley Morgan had grown up and become so handsome. And a star. I was just flabbergasted."

"I was a bit as well, Ms. Agnes." No way he was using the woman's first name. He would *not* be accused of flirting with her. But he did have to make himself not stare. Whoever did her eyebrows must've been hitting the bottle. One was nicely curved but the other was full on Vulcan. He turned his attention to Stella..

Stella beamed at him. "I was telling Billy that we should all have dinner. Let you and Agnes June get reacquainted. I was thinking Sunday would be good. If you're free."

"Oh I'm sorry, Stella. Cody's coming over Sunday to work with that new fella I hired, Bobby. She's teaching him to rope and I promised to cook her a steak."

"Well, I'm sure Cody wouldn't mind if you—"

"Oh hell yeah Cody would."

Riley had never loved Cody more than at that moment. He cut a look to his savior who was leaning on the bar behind him. "I'm not gonna cancel on you half-pint."

"Better not or there'll be hell to pay, Riley Morgan."

Riley had to fight back the smile that wanted to claim his face. "I'm sorry, Stella. You know I can't disappoint your girl."

Stella cut her eyes at Cody in a manner that told Riley that later, Stella would give her hell. Riley would gladly make recompense for whatever hell Cody caught. As nice as she might be, Agnes June was downright scary. Big over-white teeth were framed with fire-engine red lips that looked like they'd been cosmetically plumped one too many times, and set in a face that had been pulled so tight, it was a like skin stretched over bone.

"Well, there will be plenty of time once Agnes June gets settled back home."

"Oh I see Billy waving at me. Got one more set to play." Riley took a quick drink of his beer. "You ladies have a fine night."

As he hurried away, he suppressed the urge to shudder. Sadly, he'd reached the age in life where the choice of companions was slim. At least in these parts. Most women over thirty were married and those who weren't were single for a reason. Either way, it didn't leave him a lot of dateable choices.

Not that he was looking for a date. He'd had his share of those. His phone chimed and he pulled it out of his pocket. "Well I'll be damned." He stopped to type in a response, put the phone back into his pocket and grinned.

Life was just chock full of surprises.

CIANA STONE

Chapter Four

Analise stood on the sidewalk, watching the people. New Orleans was amazing. She couldn't wait to explore it more tomorrow. She'd arrived late in the afternoon and by the time she had the RV set up at the campground and gotten directions to the city, she had just enough time to arrive before dusk. New Orleans might be a city that didn't sleep, but she was tired. She'd driven all day and had not slept well last night.

She was glad she'd decided to purchase the scooter she'd bought in Tennessee. It was a cute little thing, red and shiny and as long as she didn't have to ride it far, it was great. She wouldn't want to put it on a highway, but for driving short jaunts to and from whatever campground she was in, it was perfect.

A crowd of people, obviously with a few drinks under their belts, approached and she backed up to the side of the building to let them pass. One of the women in the group stopped. "Oh, it that a voodoo doll?"

"Yes." Analise handed the woman the doll. "I got it at that shop—" she pointed down the street in the direction the group was headed.

"Cool." The woman returned it to her. "Hey, want me to take your picture with it?"

Analise smiled. "Yes, thanks."

She'd taken a ton of pictures, but taking selfies wasn't exactly her thing. She handed the woman her phone and then held the doll up beside her face, like a game show hostess displaying a prize.

"Got it!" The woman grinned and returned Analise's phone. "Have fun."

"You too." Analise accessed the photos and looked at the image. It wasn't horrible. The woman had taken a shot from the waist up and you could see the window of the bar behind Analise.

On impulse she accessed her messenger app and keyed in a message. *Voodoo Annie and her doll.* She attached the photo and hit send.

A second later she felt a minor stab of panic. She and Riley had never exchanged photos. He'd never seemed interested in what she looked like. He'd once asked why she didn't have a photo of herself on her author page on Facebook and she had explained that her husband was not a big fan of her writing. He didn't want any of his business associates running across an image of her on the Ana Lise Author Page.

He had never asked anything more about it and had displayed no interest at all in her appearance. What if he thought she was being…being what? He'd just invited her to a festival, hadn't he? That meant that at the very least they were friends. And if she went to the festival she'd meet him so it wasn't a big deal to send the photo.

Was it?

Then again, she *had* just sent a picture to a man she'd met over the internet. She thought she knew him but what if she didn't? What if he wasn't at all what he seemed? Her excitement over being in New Orleans paled as she gnawed that mental bone. Now she didn't feel much like exploring. And the idea of finding a place to eat had lost all appeal.

She felt a little sick to her stomach. She'd just sent a picture of herself to Riley. Why did that make her so nervous? Was it that she didn't trust him to be who she thought he was, or was she vain enough to be concerned that he wouldn't think her pretty?

Her phone chimed and she pulled it out to look at it. *Voodoo Annie. You must be the one with the straw hair. Who's that pretty lady with you?*

Pretty lady? Pretty? Why did that infuse her with a blast of energy and excitement, quicken not just her step but her pulse? Did it really matter what Riley thought of her looks? And maybe he was just being nice. He *was* a polite man.

God, it'd been way too long since she'd dealt with men. At least as a single woman. The last time she was with a man other than her husband she'd been ... that thought stopped her dead in her tracks. Dear god, that was more than twenty-five years ago. It'd been so long since she'd gotten attention from the opposite sex that she had completely forgotten how to deal with it.

And there she went again. *Was* he giving her attention or simply responding in a nice manner to something she'd sent? Maybe he thought she was fishing for a compliment. After all, she did send him a photo of herself. Damn it all. Maybe she was just over-thinking the whole thing

With a groan, she shoved the phone into her pocket and walked the rest of the way to her scooter, trying to figure out if she should respond and if she did, what she should say. She had not figured it out by the time she got back to the campground, rolled the scooter onto the carrier attached to the rear of the RV and locked it up for the night.

She let herself in, put her purchases on the bed and then opened the refrigerator. After pulling out makings for a salad she popped some leftover pasta into the microwave and pulled out her phone.

Katie, answered on the second ring. "So, how is 'Nawlins?"

"Amazing. I bought a voodoo doll."

"Ugh, what do you want with one of those ugly old things?"

"I have no idea. It was an impulse purchase."

"Okay, whatever. You staying in the city?"

"No, I'm back at the RV. I – I think I may have screwed up, Katie."

"What do you mean?"

Analise told her about the text, about Riley inviting her to the festival and about sending him the photo.

"So?" Katie asked when Analise finished.

"So? What do you mean so?"

"I mean what's the issue? You've been online buddies for over a year now, Analise. He knows you're traveling and he invited you to a festival. Not to his house or his bed, but to something where there will be millions of people there and—

"Millions? In a place called Cotton Creek?"

"Okay, you're right. Not millions, but at least hundreds and the point is, if you say yes and show up, he's gonna see you so what's the big deal."

"He called me pretty."

"Well you are, dummy."

Analise sighed, forgot about dinner and flopped down on the small sofa. "Well, I don't feel like it."

"Ah honey, you're just letting the rat bastard back in your head."

"No, no, I'm not. Rick never called me ugly or anything. He just … he just ignored me for the most part. At least after the first few years. The last few … well I don't know if he even realized I was around unless he needed something."

"And that's part of the reason you're better off without him. But back to you. You're really pretty Analise. You have a nice figure, not all wrinkly and scrawny and your hair still looks good so all in all you've got nothing to worry about Besides, what does he look like?"

"I don't have a clue."

"Exactly. He could look like a barrel with the middle hoop busted out."

Analise laughed. Katie had a country way of phrasing things. "Yeah, you're right. So, how should I respond?"

"I don't know. Just don't obsess about it, okay?"

"I'll try not to."

"Okay, so how long are you going to be in New Orleans?"

"A week maybe? I want to see as much as I can while I'm here."

"And then?"

41

"Then Galveston, Corpus Christie and San Antonio. I decided to go to that conference and registered this morning. Think I could crash with you a couple of days after that?"

"You know you can. And I'm so glad you decided to go to the conference. It'll be fun. You want to drive here and leave your RV and ride with me?"

"That'd be great."

"So…you going to take him up on his invitation?"

Analise leaned back and closed her eyes. "I don't know. I'll sleep on it."

"Okay. Oops, there went the bell on the stove. Gotta scoot. Call me in the morning. Love you!"

"I will and love you too."

Analise put the phone down on the couch beside her. Katie was right. She and Riley were friends and their friendship wasn't based on looks. Heck, if she really thought about it, it was founded on her asking him a million questions.

Thus far there hadn't been a lot of quid pro quo in the friendship. Unless you count the recipes she'd given him for simple meals. Apparently he wasn't much of a cook.

Still, she was reading way too much into all of this. Pushing herself up, she got focused on finishing her meal and sat down at the small table to eat. She opened a video on her Kindle and watched it as she ate. The messenger app popped open with a personal message.

It was a private message on her author fan page on Facebook. A little spark of nervousness hit her until she realized it wasn't Riley. She didn't get a lot of personal messages through her author page, so curiosity had her opening it. As he read her eyes widened.

Hi. You don't know me but I live in Cotton Creek and am a friend of Riley Morgan's. I know you are too and I thought you might enjoy this. Sorry the video is so bad. The bar was really crowded so you probably can't see him, but that's him singing. He's not bad.

Oh, I read your new book. It was good. Colt sounded a lot like Riley.

Have a good night.

Cody Sweet

Analise clicked on the link and her browser opened on a YouTube video. She could see a crowd of people in what looked like an old bar. At the far side of the room there were men on a wooden stage. Two of them were seated, each holding instruments. A third man was at the drums and at the front of the stage two men stood at the microphone, one heavyset and the other tall and lanky.

She couldn't make out their features, and people kept moving in front of the camera, but she could hear the music despite the crowd. She listened and then listened again. Which one was Riley? Was he the stocky guy or the lanky one?

Whoever he was, he was part of music that brought a smile to her face. When she finally turned it off, she sat at the table, staring at the phone. Who was Cody Sweet and why would she send this? Male or female? Probably female because of the reference to the book. Not many men read romances.

On impulse she clicked on Cody's profile name. When the page loaded she sat back in her chair. Cody was definitely a female. A beautiful one. Analise cruised through the page but there were no other photos on it aside from horses and a couple of shots that look like they'd been taken in the bar.

Just what kind of friend was this Cody?

Analise accessed the message app again to respond.

Hi Cody,

First, thank you for taking the time to read my book. I hope you enjoyed it.

I was surprised to get your message. Yes, Riley and I are friends. Well, Facebook friends. We've never actually met. He's been a great help to me when I have questions about ranching, horses and that sort of thing

The music was great and I really enjoyed it. Thanks for sharing it with me and for your message.

Best,

Ana Lise

She hesitated for a moment. Should she use her real name. Ana Lise was what she published under, but Riley knew her real name. She changed it to Analise and then hit send. Rather than just sitting there, waiting to see if there would be another message, she cleaned up and then showered and got ready for bed. She checked the phone and didn't see a message so put the phone on the charger, double checked to make sure the doors were locked and climbed into bed.

The problem was, she wasn't sleepy. Her mind kept jumping from her texts with Riley to the message from his friend Cody to the music she heard. Which man in the video was Riley? Was he tall or stocky?

Her hands moved up in the dark to cover her face. His friend Cody had recognized Riley in Analise's fictional character Colt? Had she been that obvious, and did Cody realize that Analise had fashioned a man with the physical appearance she found appealing and then assigned him all of the qualities she liked in Riley?

That thought tortured her for a good hour until she threw off her bedcovers, got up to get her Kindle and then went back to bed. She searched through her library and selected an old Western. It was one of her favorites and she'd watched it more times than she could count.

When the hero of the film came on screen she smiled. Nate Bridges. God, she'd had such a crush on that man. Tall and lean, he had warm brown hair that tended to curl just a bit at the ends when he wore it long. His eyes were hazel but could appear blue if he had on a blue shirt and his smile could light up not just a room but a continent.

Analise snuggled into a more comfortable position and let herself get lost in the movie. Before long her eyes started to get heavy and she drifted off into a dream where she was the damsel being rescued by the rough and rowdy desperado with a heart of gold.

Chapter Five

Riley stepped out onto the front porch with a steaming mug of coffee in his hand. After nearly two months of drought, last night a storm had rolled through that rocked the house. According to the local news, more than a couple of tornados had spawned from the storm.

There were no reports yet on damage or loss of life. Power had gone out and the generator supplied just enough juice to keep the refrigerator and freezer running and his phone charged. It wasn't the first night he'd spent without lights or the company of the television and probably wouldn't be the last.

Cody had texted to check on him and let him know she was okay. He'd also heard from Analise. She was in Galveston and from the sounds of it, enjoying sightseeing. She also mentioned that she'd been taking time to work on the wooden chest she had bought before she left New Jersey. On days she didn't feel like sightseeing, she'd work on it.

He smiled at the thought. She was dead set on finishing that thing and doing a good job. He admired anyone who saw a task through to the end, and liked that she seemed to be one of those people.

From where he sat, he looked out over his land. There appeared to be some branches down, but it didn't look like there was damage to any of the structures. He'd count himself lucky that there hadn't been any tornados in his neck of the woods.

His phone rang. He pulled it out of his pocket and looked at the caller ID. before answering..

"Morning, Cody. Everything okay out your way?

"Yeah. Had a tree come down across one of the fences, but we don't have anything in that section of pasture so it can wait. How 'bout you?"

"Everything's fine. You hear from your mama this morning?"

"Yep. They're fine. But Otis has a mess. Twister took off half his roof."

Riley grimaced. Otis Caskey ran the local barbershop and a nicer man never walked the planet. His wife Pearl ran a cash register at the local grocery. They made ends meet but weren't what you'd call affluent.

"Anyone over there helping Otis?"

"Part of why I called. Soon as I get this tree taken care of I'm headed over. Dad's on his way now, along with Jimmy and Frank Odel. Frank's closing the feed store for the day. You think you can pitch in?"

"You know it. What can I bring?"

"Extra hands if you can spare 'em."

"I'll bring the kid with me."

"Thanks. See you there."

Riley's next call was to Bobby who answered on the first ring. "How 'bout taking a ride to town with me, Bobby? Otis got some damage to his roof in the storm and we're gonna help him out."

"I'll be in the truck in three minutes."

A smile crossed Riley's face. Bobby might have more questions than a round of Jeopardy but the boy had heart. He went back inside to put his coffee mug in the sink, but as an afterthought, dug out two of those metal travel cups and filled them with coffee. He dumped several spoons of sugar into one for Bobby.

After cramming his hat on his head and getting his keys, he carried both cups outside. Sure enough, Bobby was standing beside Riley's truck.

"Coffee?" Riley handed him the one laced with sugar.

"Thank you, sir."

"My pleasure." Riley climbed in the truck and started it as Bobby hurried around to get into the passenger's side.

"Mr. Odel's place a mess?"

"Don't know. Cody called and said half the roof got torn off by a twister."

"That was one hell of a storm wasn't it? We were lucky. Buckets of rain though. But I guess that's good, huh?"

"We need all the rain we can get, but a downpour like that isn't exactly friendly to crops. Can beat 'em down pretty bad."

"I didn't think about that. Folks around here depend a lot on those crops, don't they?"

"Yeah, Bobby, they do. It's what makes 'em a living."

"So what happens if their crops get wiped out? How do they survive?"

Riley cut a look over at him. "They either get by on what they have saved, or by the kindness of family and friends, or they don't make it."

Bobby nodded and looked out of the window for a while. "I don't like to think of folks losing their homes."

"Neither do I."

"But you help them out, Mr. Morgan. I know you do. Cody told me how you helped her family when her dad got hurt, and how you helped old Mr. Eastman when he broke his hip and couldn't work his cotton farm."

"I've been luckier than some so I try and pay it forward a bit. Besides, it's what you do when you're part of a community. You help each other out."

"That's how I want to be. One day I want to have my own place. Maybe raise some cotton, have some cows. Live a good life and help folks out."

"That's a nice goal, Bobby. Real nice."

"And I want to compete in the rodeo."

Riley smiled at him. "That's what I hear. Roping, right?"

"Yes, sir. Cody's been teaching me."

"She's says you have potential."

Bobby grinned. "She's real nice. Say, do you think she's too old for me?"

Riley nearly choked on his coffee. "As in to date?"

"Yeah."

"Well, yes, I do. Bobby. You're what, twenty-two?"

"Yes sir. Twenty-three in March."

"Right and she's – she's a few years older Besides, I don't think Cody's looking for a fella."

"Oh." Bobby nodded. "Now it make sense. I wondered why I never saw her with any men. Funny though, I wouldn't have thought she was a lesbian."

This time Riley spewed coffee, choked and wheezed for a bit. When he finally caught his breath he spoke. "She's not a lesbian."

"Oh! Oh, when you said she's not looking for a fella I thought you meant—"

"I just meant she's not looking to get involved with anyone."

"Oh. Oh, okay. Well, maybe one day she will be. And who knows, one day when I've won all these ribbons and belt buckles and I'm one of those guys that people say 'hey, look, that's Bobby Daniels, rodeo champion ' – maybe then she'd think twice."

Riley just shook his head, "Well, you never know do you, Bobby?"

"No, sir you never do."

Riley smiled. In some ways he envied Bobby. There was a time when he had the dreams of youth, the 'pie-in-the-sky dreams' as his father called them. And look what happened. His dreams had come true. He'd found fame and fortune and what had it netted him? He'd spent half a life chasing skirts and being chased, of making insane amounts of money and wasting most of it and here he was, back where he'd started. Those dreams of his youth had been realized and tarnished by his own bad choices.

And the saddest part was he didn't seem to have any more dreams.

*****

Analise smiled as she read the text from Cody. It was odd, but since that first message Cody had sent her, they had been messaging and texting every day. It had been a month since that first text and now Analise felt like she'd made a new friend.

Cody was much younger, but what a spirited and independent woman she was. She seemed so self-confident and comfortable in her own skin and could laugh at her own short-comings.

Like not being able to cook. Analise had literally laughed out loud reading about Cody's attempt to make a Beef Wellington for her sisters, Riley and some guy named Bobby. It had been such a disaster that they ended up roasting hotdogs over an open fire and eating them sans buns with cold canned beans.

Despite the cooking fiasco, it sounded like fun to Analise and she admired Cody's ability to bounce back and not let it get her down.

Can't wait to meet you in person. She typed as she got out of the hotel elevator on her floor. *Headed to my room to shower and change. Big formal dress dinner tonight and I found a really pretty dress at a local shop.*

Send pictures! Was the response she received. *And have fun!*

Will do! Analise replied and inserted the keycard into her room's door. She looked up as she stepped into the room and froze. The room was in shambles. Her belongings were scattered all over the floor, along with the bedcovers. Analise just stood there and stared in disbelief for a few seconds before panic set in. Her eyes darted one direction and then another. Was there someone still in the room? Her heart hammered in her chest.

Careful not to make a sound she eased to the bathroom door. The room was empty. Analise crept into the bedroom.

Like the bathroom it was empty. Relief washed through her until a thought dawned.

Her laptop!

One glance told her it was no longer on the small table in the corner. Her eyes darted to the armoire containing the television and then to the dresser. Nothing. With rising panic she threw herself onto her hands and knees and started sorting through the mess on the floor.

Ten minutes later, having gone through the entire room, piling sheets and bed pillows back onto the bed and tossing clothing into her travel case in the closet, she admitted defeat. Her laptop and Kindle were not in the room!

There was nothing else to do but pick up the hotel phone and call the manager. She did just that. Ten minutes that seemed like an hour later, a manager arrived.

"Mrs. Becke, I understand you have a problem?"

"Yes, you might call it that. I returned to my room just –" She checked the clock on the nightstand. "Just twenty minutes ago and found my room trashed. My belongings and the bed clothes were all over the floor and the drawers, my luggage and even the bathroom have been searched and things scattered."

He took a look around the room, peeked into the bathroom and then the closet. "So, your clothes were not in the closet when you returned?"

"No, they were on the floor. I picked everything up. And my laptop and my Kindle are missing."

"I see. I'm very sorry for this, Mrs. Becke. That *is* the reason we provide room safes. It's a shame you didn't take advantage of it. Are you sure you didn't leave the laptop and Kindle somewhere else in the hotel? I noticed you were registered for the convention."

Until that moment, Analise had been on the verge of tears. His comment about the safe came across a bit condescending and rankled her. "I shouldn't have to put things in a safe to keep them from getting stolen. And no. I didn't have them with me. I was working on a book this morning and left it right there." She pointed to the table in the corner of the room.

"Yes, I see. Well, as I said, I am very sorry and will definitely look into this right away. I will have security look over the video surveillance from the hallway. Unfortunately we have no other vacancies, so I'm unable to switch your room. Of course we can contact the police if you wish. And naturally the front desk will issue you a new keycard immediately.I do suggest you contact your insurance carrier – providing you had the items insured."

Analise wanted to smack him. He acted as if she'd just reported a tube of lipstick had been stolen and his entire demeanor was supercilious "Well, insurance is hardly going to cover the cost of my book files that were on that laptop."

"Yes, I do understand but you did, of course, have a backup."

Suddenly she wanted to kiss the man. Why had she been in such a panic? Her files were all on her One Drive cloud storage as well as backed up on DropBox and she had a backup subscription that automatically backed up her entire system and files every day.

"Oh yes, yes, I do. Thank you for looking into this for me."

"My pleasure. We will do everything we can to retrieve the missing items. If we have failed to do so by the end of your stay, please come see me and I will see what we can do to make reparations."

"Thank you. I appreciate that."

"Excellent. Remember to stop by the desk for a new keycard."

"Yes. I will." Analise followed him to the door and locked it behind him. The first order of business was to get online on her phone and change her passwords for every online account and membership. Her laptop was password protected, but people were a lot smarter these days than ever. Anything could be hacked.

Once that was done, she took another look around. She was still upset but there wasn't anything she could do – aside from letting it ruin her last night at the convention. Analise was determined not to let that happen.

Despite wanting to call Katie and have her stand guard, Analise told herself to 'woman up' and headed for the shower. She washed up, did her hair and makeup then returned to the bedroom and opened the closet door to take out the dress she'd purchased.

"Well shit."

How had she not noticed that everything on hangers had been damaged? It looked like someone had taken a knife and systematically sliced every article of clothing. That made her look at her travel case where she'd piled the clothes that were left in the floor.

"Shit, shit, shit!" Aside from the slacks and blouse she'd just taken off, not one piece of clothing had escaped destruction.

Analise redressed in what she'd taken off and grabbed her phone. Her first call was to the police. This went beyond a simple robbery. It felt like an attack or a threat. It took her ten minutes with the dispatcher who promised to have an officer to her within half an hour. Analise's next call was to Katie.

"You ready?" Katie asked rather than saying hello.

"Not quite. I – I had a little problem."

"Now don't you start. I know that dress is a little sexier than you originally wanted but it looks fantastic on you and—"

"My room was trashed. All of my stuff was destroyed."

"What?"

"When I got back to my room it'd been trashed. My laptop and Kindle are gone and all my clothes have been cut up."

"Do. Not. Move. I'm on my way."

Analise couldn't help but smile. One thing about Katie was that she was there for a friend through thick and thin. She no more had time to get her purse and phone before there was a tap at the door.

Katie threw her arms around Analise. "Are you okay? Oh honey, this is awful. Just awful. Did you call the manager? What about the police?"

Analise thought she'd been doing well until that moment. All at once she felt tears gather and she clung to Katie for a moment. She fought to get herself composed and then pulled back.

"Yes. He's already been here. Now don't fret, okay? It's just stuff. It can all be replaced. And so what if I don't dress up for the dinner? I have jeans and stuff in the RV. After the police come I'll just take my case and go down to get what I need for tonight and tomorrow." That sounded like a strong, independent woman. She was amazed she'd pulled it off and that her nose hadn't grown several inches. Inside she was a quivering bunch of nerves.

"Screw the event. That lunatic could be out there, lurking in the hotel. My god, someone sliced up your clothing. You can't stay in this room Analise. You're moving in with me."

That was the most welcome offer Katie could have made. Analise knew she'd never sleep a wink in that room.

"Sure I can."

"No. No. We're not going."

"Katie, you've been looking forward to this for-"

"I said we're not going. We'll get you moved into my room as soon as the police leave. Where are they by the way?"

"They'll be here any time."

"Well good. Honey, this thing feels like a threat. And that doesn't make any sense. Why would someone – oh my god. Rick! Analise do you think he set this up? He was really mad about you taking that money. What if—"

"No. He wouldn't do something like this."

"You sure? That recording you sent me sounded pretty bad. You even said your attorney listened to it and said it was threatening. And if you really think he's in bed with some bad people then—"

"Katie, no." Analise couldn't let her mind go there. Rick might be upset with her, but he'd never arrange for something like this.

"Well, someone has a grudge against you for something. You don't have any psycho fans, do you?

"Not that I know of."

Just then a knock sounded at the door. Analise and Katie looked at one another and then Analise called out. "Yes?"

"San Antonio police."

She looked through the peephole on the door. There were two uniformed officers standing outside the door, one male and one female. She opened it and stepped back. "Thank you for coming."

They walked in and noticed Katie. Analise quickly introduced Katie and launched into an explanation on what had happened. She expected them to write it down, have her sign a form and be done with it.

She did not expect them to call in a crime tech unit to dust for fingerprints and gather evidence. The seriousness they displayed made her nervousness grow into full-blown fear. By the time the crime techs and left, she was close to the end of her rope. They'd taken her belongings with them as evidence, leaving her only with the clothes on her back, her purse and her phone.

"Thank you so much." Analise said to the two officers. "And I hate to ask but would you consider going with me to the parking lot? My RV is there and I need to get some clothes."

"It's probably be smart for us the check your vehicle." The female officer said.

"I'll go with you," Katie volunteered.

Analise gave her a grateful smile and accompanied by the officers went to the parking lot. The officers checked around the vehicle and tested the doors. All were locked. Still, they entered before Analise and checked the interior.

"Doesn't appear to have been tampered with." The male officer announced. "Would you like for us to wait and escort you back into the hotel."

Analise wanted to say yes, but she was trying not to let this thing turn her into a sniveling coward. "No. Thank you. We'll be fine."

The promised to let her know if the investigation turned up anything, gave her a copy of the report and left. "Okay, so what do you need?" Katie asked.

Analise turned her attention to gathering clothing, found a couple of pairs of jeans, clean underwear and blouses. "This will do."

"Okay, then. Let's head back and check your room once more for anything the police didn't take and then get you settled into my room."

"Thanks, Katie. I owe you."

"No you don't. Oh by the way, you remember Alice Sheraton?"

"The redhead who writes romantic suspense?"

"Yes. She said the book signing tomorrow was going to be pretty good."

"Oh?" Analise stepped outside and waited for Katie to exit.

"Yeah, the convention ran ads in the local papers and on the radio. They're expecting a pretty big crowd and there's close to eighty reads already registered for the convention."

"Is that good?" Analise made sure the door was locked.

"Hell yeah." Katie fell into step with her as Analise headed for the hotel.

"Well that's good. But the signing? How many books do I need? I only have twenty. I do have some postcards with QR codes for the ebook. You think that will be okay?"

"Better to run out than have a butt-load unsold sitting on your table."

"Good point." Analise stopped walking. "Should I go ahead and get the books and stuff out of the RV?"

"No, we can scoot down here in the morning."

"You sure? I don't want you to feel you have to—"

"Hush. I mean it. You're my friend and after what happened."

That's when the reality of it hit, really hit. Analise felt her whole body tremble and fought not to burst into tears. She tried to get herself under control but tears started to stream down her face. She felt Katie's hand on her arm and stopped.

Katie put her arms around Analise and hugged her. "The police will figure it out honey. You're safe now. They didn't touch your RV so maybe it was just random, you know?"

Analise latched onto Katie's statement like a lifeline. She was right. Why in the world would someone break into her room like that? Things like this probably happen all the time. Just a random act. It wasn't personal. If it had been the attacker would have broken into her RV.

In the grander scheme of things, this was just a bump in the road. She could afford to buy a new laptop and Kindle, and maybe the hotel would even help on that. But whatever the case, it would be okay.

She wasn't about to let anything spoil her escape, and her new start on life.

"Earth to Analise."

It was then she realized that not only had they made it to the hotel and Katie had been chatting away and she hadn't heard a word. "Oh, sorry. I'm sorry."

"It's okay." Katie pointed to the door.

"Sorry."

"No worries hon." Katie opened the door and held it for Analise.

They made it to the elevator and up to the fourth floor without encountering anyone they knew, and Analise was grateful for that. She was in no mood to be sociable at the moment. When they reached her room, her hand trembled trying to insert the key card. She dropped it and Katie knelt to pick it up.

"Here, let me get this." She unlocked and opened the door, stepping in ahead of Analise.

The room was empty, but still Analise felt uncomfortable. She made a quick survey of the room. There was a pair of shoes in the closet, her cosmetics bag and toiletries in the bathroom and her shampoo and conditioner in the shower.

She and Katie gathered up everything and headed for Katie's room. Analise breathed a little easier once they were safely in the room with the door locked.

"Just put your bathroom stuff on the vanity and I'll put your clothes in one of the drawers."

"I hope the police return my luggage." Analise commented over her shoulder as she headed for the bathroom.

"They will honey."

Analise glanced at the clock between the two queen beds as she returned to the bedroom. "Katie you better start getting ready."

"Oh, I'm not going."

"Yes, you are."

"No. I'm staying here with you. Will find a place that delivers and have a pajama party."

"No. Seriously. No. You have that pretty dress you bought just for the event. I want you to go. I'll stay here. Take some notes or something. There's bound to be –" She looked around the room. "Yes, there's a pad and pen right there."

"Analise, I'm not leaving you alone."

"I really want you to go. I – I need some time to myself. Please?"

"Well. If you're sure."

"I am. Thank you so much for letting me stay with you."

"Are you sure you want to be by yourself?"

"I am. I'm – I just feel tired."

61

"Okay sugar, if that's what you want."

"It is, now go get gussied up."

Katie smiled. "All righty."

As Katie headed for the bathroom, Analise took a seat at the small table in front of the window. Katie's room was on the front of the hotel. Directly across the street was the Alamo. Analise watched the people who were visiting the historic landmark. The first time she saw it, the day she arrived, she was surprised how small it was. History made it seem so huge. Or maybe it was fiction based on history that did that.

Writers had a way of romanticizing places they wrote about. Her thoughts turned to the book she was working on. She picked up the pen from the table and slid the notepad in front of her to jot down a line. Maybe she should set it in this area. The break-in sparked ideas. San Antonio might have a seedy underbelly that would work well as a backdrop.

Maybe the book would be more of a romantic suspense. Her hero could own a ranch in the county – she'd have to research what county this was.

She picked up her phone, accessed the browser and ran a search. *Bejar County*. She jotted on the note pad. Wonder how that was pronounced. Another Google search provided the answer. *Bear*. She added that to her notes.

Maybe on special occasions he'd drive into San Antonio. Have dinner at a place like this. Maybe he'd witness something happening. A woman getting attacked. Or finding a woman unconscious in the parking lot.

As she thought about it, her hero appeared in her mind as Nate Bridges. Analise smiled. Back in New York, she'd never told any of the women she knew about her fan crush.

She doubted any of them had watched his westerns. He was a popular actor in several other roles, and while she liked them, it was his portrayal of the western hero that really revved her engine.

Katie agreed that Nate was fine with a capital F. Too bad it was a fantasy. There were no more real down-to-earth guys left, which is why Analise had blended the fantasy man with Riley's personality and cooked up the perfect hero.

Well, perfect to her. And completely unattainable. That thought gave her pause. Was that what she wanted? Had she been trying to make Riley into some make-believe romantic hero because she was unhappy with her life?

She hoped not. As nice a fantasy as it would be, she had no hopes that when she actually met him that sparks would fly, angels would sing and love would explode between them. That was something she'd be able to use in her romance writing, but not something that could happen in real life.

In real life, she was just a woman without a clue about what she really wanted and how she was going to figure that out.

Chapter Six

It took less time than Riley anticipated to get the pig into the pit. But with him and Deputy Tom Greene there to help, Billy and Cody's job had been easier. Riley stood outside, staring up at the sky, watching the sun fade into the horizon. Cody and Billy had gone inside the bar to get beer and Tom was checking in with the station.

Riley kept checking his phone for messages. Nothing. He'd been expecting Analise to roll in early that afternoon but she hadn't shown up, nor had she texted. He was starting to get a little concerned. In his experience, she was the type of person who did what she said she'd do. If she said she would text at a certain time, he could set his watch by it.

He'd been a little surprised when she said she was going to arrive before the end of September and hoped that wasn't a problem. Her friend, Katie, was currently staying with her sister due to some vandalism at her home while Analise was visiting and Analise didn't have anywhere else to go in the state.

Riley had assured her it would be fine. There was a pig roasting every week at Billy's and you couldn't tell much difference between a regular Saturday night at the bar and the festival weekend since it was always the same people who came to both.

Tom walked over as Riley's fingers hovered over the keypad. "There's been an accident at the town limits. An RV. I need to—"

"An RV?" Riley was a bit surprised at the way his gut clenched. Analise was driving an RV. "Is it serious?"

"Don't know. Helen over at the station just gave me the call."

"Mind if I ride with you? I'm expecting a friend to come into town."

"A friend who drives an RV?"

"Yep."

"Well sure, come on."

"Let me tell Billy." Riley called Billy and as soon as Billy answered, Riley filled him in. He climbed into the cruiser with Tom and they headed to the opposite end of town. That took all of three minutes.

Sure enough an RV was stopped right in the road. "Is that..." Tom leaned closer to the windshield, peering at the vehicle.

"An engine?" Riley was as surprised as Tom because it sure as heck looked like the whole engine block was sitting on the pavement beneath the vehicle.

"Well you don't see that every day." Tom stopped and got out of the cruiser.

Riley followed suit and it was then he noticed the woman standing beside the driver's door of the RV. She wasn't a tall woman, maybe a bit taller than Cody but with a knock-out build and dark brown hair a little bit longer than shoulder length.

It had to be Analise. He and Tom approached the vehicle and she turned toward them.

*****

Analise felt like the bottom had dropped out of more than her RV. What in the world was she going to do now? Could it be repaired? She had to be able to get it to a

65

campground so she'd have somewhere to stay, but if the engine wasn't in the darn thing nothing inside would work.

She was royally screwed and mad. There had been too many mishaps lately. After the convention, on the way to Katie's house the RV had started making groaning noises. Once she got to Katie's she'd gotten on Katie's computer and looked up repair places. She took it to one and they said they couldn't find anything wrong.

Then Katie's house was vandalized. Someone threw a brick through the glass of the front door. That had really freaked Katie out. It didn't do Analise's nerves much good either since she'd been dealing with trying to get the RV checked at the time.

What she'd paid that mechanic was obviously three hundred dollars wasted. She felt like cursing, but instead was running a Google search on tow trucks and mechanics.

She heard the car pull up p and after a moment she stopped what she was doing, turned and glanced at the men who were approaching. The one in the lead was medium height with a lean wiry build, curly blond hair and wore a badge on his shirt.

The other was tall and lanky, wearing faded jeans, boots and a cowboy hat. And was Nate Bridges!. She stared speechlessly as the men approached.

"Analise?" Nate Bridges asked.

"Uh, yes?"

"It's me. Riley."

Analise's mind went into a whirl that had her reaching for the side of the RV. She felt like a top being spun. Everything was swirling around her and Nate Bridges was reaching for her. She couldn't focus, couldn't think.

*****

"Oh hell," Riley caught her as she fell and lifted her into his arms. She hung there, limp.

"Maybe you better run her over to Doc's." Tom suggested.

"Billy's is closer. Call Doc and have him meet us there."

"Will do."

Riley started in the direction of Billy's house, which was less than a block away. Hannah was just getting out of her car when he strode into the yard. "Oh my god! Riley, what happened?"

"Woman passed out. Can I use your sofa?"

"Of course!" Hannah hurried up the front steps to open the door, yelling for her mother. "Mama! Call Doc. Someone's hurt."

Stella ran into the front room as Riley was easing Analise onto the sofa. "What happened?"

"Her vehicle broke down in town. Tom and I went to check it out and when we walked up she fainted."

"Let me get a cool cloth. Be right back." Stella hurried off.

"I'll get water and call Doc." Hannah hurried off as well.

Riley didn't quite know what to do, so he sat on the edge of the sofa beside Analise. She was prettier in person than in the photo she'd sent with her and the voodoo doll. He knew she was in her early 40's but she looked younger.

As he watched her, her eyes fluttered and opened. The moment her gaze landed on him her eyes flew open wide and she gasped. "Oh my God."

"Are you okay? Do you hurt anywhere?"

"Here honey." Stella hurried in with a cool cloth and placed it on Analise's forehead. "Now you just lie still 'til the doctor gets here. You want some water?"

"No. Thank you."

"Okay. I'll be on the porch watching for the doctor. Riley you yell if she needs anything, hear?"

"Yes ma'am." He turned his gaze from Stella to Analise. "You okay, Annie?"

Analise couldn't form any more words. Her brain simply wasn't prepared to see Nate Bridges sitting there looking at her. This had to be a dream. Oh god, what if she had been in an accident and was hallucinating as her body was shutting down. Was she dying? That made her break out in shivers and a sweat at the same time.

"Analise, are you okay? Can you talk?"

She managed to shake her head back and forth in quick jerks. Nate reached to take her hand. "Squeeze my hand if you understand."

Squeeze my hand? For the love of God, she could barely breathe. Nate Bridges was holding her hand.

"Listen to me. It's Riley. You're in Cotton Creek and your rig broke down. You fainted. But you're safe. I just need you to squeeze my hand if you understand what I'm saying."

Blood must have returned to her brain, or her neurons had started firing again because she had least had the where-with-all to follow his instructions. She squeezed his hand and was rewarded with a smile that literally took her breath away.

But it couldn't be real. Her friend Riley was a rancher in a small town, a man who had cattle and played in a little hometown band and made furniture. The man sitting beside her, holding her hand was a movie star.

The longer she lay there staring at him, the more questions her mind conjured up. Why was he playing this game with her? Where was she and why was he pretending to be her friend, Riley? Finally curiosity overpowered shock and she opened her mouth. "Who *are* you?"

"Riley. Analise it's me, Riley Morgan."

"No." She pulled her hand away from his and pushed into a sitting position. "No, you're not Riley. You're …. You're …"

"Riley."

"No!" She pushed him out of the way so she could stand. "My friend Riley isn't … isn't …"

"Isn't what?" He stood to face her, forcing her to tilt her head back to look up and meet his eyes.

"Isn't you!"

"Well, if I'm not me then who am I?" God help her it *was* Nate Bridges. She'd listened to that voice a thousand times.

"You know who you are. You're him."

"Him who?"

"Nate Bridges!"

Riley physically stepped back at that. He didn't know whether to turn tail and run, lie to her face or fess up and tell the truth. For a few moments they just stared at one another. Her with her fists clenched by her sides, face flushed and her chest rising and falling rapidly – and him feeling like the last tin can standing on the wall at target practice.

Finally he blew out his breath, swept off his hat and ran his hand back through his hair. "I'm not Nate Bridges, Analise. At least not anymore. And my real name *is* Riley Morgan. I haven't been Nate Bridges in a long time."

He could tell that she wasn't buying it by the way she shook her head and held her hands up in front of her like she was warding off an attacker. "No. Oh no. This can't be happening. You can't be Riley."

"Well sure I can, Annie." He gave her a smile. "The same Riley who told you how to stain your treasure box, and what calving season is and –"

"Oh. My. God." She took a step back. "You're him. I mean it is you. But you're him, too."

"Yeah, I guess I am."

Analise didn't know why but all of a sudden she was furious. Maybe it was precipitated by embarrassment. She had just gushed, after all, like a star-struck teenager. And God only knew that if the energy of the fantasies she'd had about Nate Bridges were turned to fuel, she could power a damn nuclear submarine.

And then there was the fact that he hadn't bothered to tell her that he was a freaking movie star.

"Well you could've been honest about it."

"Pardon?"

"About who you really are? I mean here for over a year I thought I was talking with some rancher from Bumfuck, Texas. Some guy who for whatever reason didn't have a family and was all alone, but knew a lot about ranching and making furniture and who was polite and kind and made me laugh and someone who-"

"Hold on there, Turbo, you might want to take a breath."

As much as she hated it, that sounded exactly like her friend Riley. She threw up her hands and made a loud roaring sound. "Do *not* be cute with me, Riley Morgan. I mean it. I thought you were just a regular guy, someone who was my friend and someone I'd come to care about."

"Well, I appreciate that, Annie, and I thought we were friends too."

"But not good enough friends to tell me the truth about who you are? Seriously. You invited me here. Surely you had to have known I would recognize you? For Christ's sakes, you're Nate Fucking Bridges!"

His jaw tightened and his eyes narrowed, and for the life of her she couldn't help but see Nate Bridges as he'd appear on film, that look he'd get right before he ripped into someone. It both excited and terrified her. Without being aware of it, she took two steps back and bumped into the couch.

Riley's saw the fear on her face and it smothered the irritation gnawing at him. In a way she was right. He had deliberately kept that part of his life secret from her. But in his own defense, she was just a woman he chatted with online so what did he really owe her? That thought boosted his resolve not to feel guilty, but the fear on her face and the way she moved away from him cut right through his indignation.

"I'm sorry, Annie. You're right. I am Nate. At least that's my stage name. But I left that life behind almost a decade ago and now I'm just Riley. I didn't set out to deceive you, but honestly, I didn't know you. We're internet friends and you – well you could have been anyone for all I knew."

She crossed her arms in front of her chest, a move he'd seen more than once in his life and one that spelled trouble. When a woman did that, it was a pretty sure bet she wasn't letting whatever you were saying get in.

"Well, maybe so." Her words surprised him. "But … but God in heaven, it's sure not what I expected when I came here to meet my *internet* buddy."

Riley chuckled. "I guess not."

"So what now?"

"Pardon?"

"What now? I mean, I don't even know what to say to you. You might be plain old Riley to yourself but when I look at you I see Nate Bridges."

"And I can't be both?" Hell fire. Was his past going to screw up their friendship?

"Well … well yes, of course. I mean you are, but it's different for me. I came here expecting to meet a middle-aged man with a kind heart, a good sense of humor and probably sporting a Texas- sized beer belly and not much hair."

That gave Riley a chuckle. "So you're saying I'm a disappointment?"

"Oh screw you, Riley. You know that's not what I'm saying. I'm saying that it's hard to be normal around a heart-throb movie star."

He shouldn't have let the heart-throb bit pump his ego but it did a bit. It'd been a while since a woman saw him in that light. "But I'm not anymore."

Her stance changed. The defenses came down, along with her arms. "You are to me."

The moment the words were out of her mouth looked away, towards the window.

A few seconds later, the sound of feet pounding up the steps had her turning her gaze toward the front door. It banged open and the dark-haired woman skidded to a stop in the room, breathing hard. She looked from Riley to Analise.

"Analise?"

"Yes."

"I'm Cody."

That brought the first smile to her face since she'd entered Cotton Creek. "Cody!" She ran to meet her and they collided in a bouncing, dancing hug. When they broke apart, Cody eyed her and grinned.

"Oh my god, I thought you'd be taller!"

"I thought you would too!"

"I haz a big aura." Cody grinned and cut her eyes at Riley. "What's up with you?"

"Nothing."

"Nothing? Then why're you scowling?"

"I'm not."

"Like hell. Okay, someone said something about an accident but ya'll look okay so what gives?"

"My RV broke down."

"Oh shit. Where?"

"At the edge of town."

"Well shit. Riley, did you call Jimmy?"

"No, I —"

"Well damn, why not?" She looked at Analise. "Jimmy Johnson. Yeah, really. Just like the Nascar racer. Anyway, he owns the body shop and he can fix anything."

"I don't know if he can fix this."

"Why? You didn't total it did you?"

"No. The engine fell out."

Cody looked from her to Riley and back to her. "Say what?"

"The engine fell out."

"As in fell out?"

"As in laying on the pavement fell out." Riley offered.

"Well damn. Still, Riley call Jimmy and tell him to get it and take it to his place. If it can be fixed then Jimmy can fix it. Now, where were you planning on staying, Analise?"

"Is there a hotel here?"

"Nope."

"Oh, well, I'd planned on staying in my RV."

"Not gonna happen. You'll stay with me at the ranch."

"Cody I can't put you out like—"

"You're not. You'll stay with me and that's that. Now where are your things?"

"In the RV."

"Riley—"

"Cody, quit ordering me around."

Cody slammed her mouth closed and threw her hands on her hips. A second later she looked toward the front door."I can hear you Mama."

Stella and Hannah eased around from the front door. "We didn't want to interrupt." Hannah said. "You and Riley—"

"Her and Riley what?" Cody asked.

Stella and Hannah looked at one another and then at Riley. "Well?" Cody asked. "Will someone please tell me what's going on?"

Riley slammed his hat on his head. "Annie didn't realize I used to act."

"Oooooh." Cody drew out the word for a good three seconds and then frowned. "Why'd you call her Annie?"

"She looks like an Annie."

"Oooooh." Another drawn out syllable had Analise noticing the way Stella and Hannah glanced at one another and then at Cody. That look said something but what? She made a mental note to ask Cody later.

"Yes. He neglected to share that irrelevant bit of information."

"Oooh sarcasm. I love it." Cody laughed and looped her arm across the top of Analise's shoulders. "Come on.

Walk with me over to the bar. W'll take my truck and get your stuff from your camper and take it to the ranch."

"But I called Doc." Hannah said.

"She's fine." Cody dismissed it but then looked at Analise. "I mean, you are, aren't you?"

"Yes. Quite."

"Well, all righty then. Riley, you're calling Jimmy, right?"

"Yep."

"Okay, then we'll see y'all later."

With that she turned Analise and steered her out of the door. Once they were on the sidewalk, Analise looked over at her. "Jesus, Cody. He's Nate Fucking Bridges!"

Cody burst out laughing. "Ah ha! I knew it. You have a thing for him, don't you?"

"Who? Riley or Nate?"

"Well both, but since you never saw Riley before, let's say Nate. He does it for you doesn't he?"

Analise blew out a breath. "You have no idea."

Chapter Seven

Rodrick's father, Robert, waited until dinner was concluded and the men were in his private study with brandy and cigars. He closed the door and took a seat in front of the fireplace. Rodrick and Rolf settled onto the sofa.

"Rodrick, as you know we've run into a spot of trouble." Robert opened the conversation.

His father's description annoyed him. It was more than a spot of trouble."You mean the FTC charges."

"Precisely. It appears that indictments will be handed down and there's a strong possibility that we could suffer – what did you call it Rolf?"

"A raid." The expression on Rolf's face heightened his irritation.

"Who would—"

"Department of Justice."

"You mean the FBI?" Rodrick struggled to keep the fear out of his voice despite the desperation that tightened around his chest

"Yes."

That word echoed like a death knell in his head and Rodrick turned his attention to this father. "The last time we spoke you assured me that you and Rolf had things under control and that even if indictments were issued, we were protected. Is that still the case?"

"Not entirely." Robert dragged on his cigar and exhaled a billowing plume of smoke. "Unfortunately, we can't prevent them from tracing certain transactions. Rolf is working to hide what we can, but if they look – and they will – there will be evidence that incriminates us."

"I hope you have a plan."

"We do."

"We?"

"Rolf and I have been discussing this at length for some time. We must preserve the company at all costs. That's priority number one. Just as we must insure that our more – shall we say – volatile clients see the return of their investments. But as your brother pointed out we also have to give the Feds something or someone to hang their hat on. Someone to, as is said in the movies, take the fall. "For the greater good, of course."

"You mean Rolf."

"No, Rodrick. I mean you."

"Me? Why me? Rolf's the one responsible for bringing in gangsters. Let him take the fall. Or you."

"I'm too old and have a long-standing reputation. And Rolf has children."

"As do I."

"One. In college. Rolf's family is much younger. They need their father at home. He needs to be there with his wife. Unless I've been misinformed, your wife has left you."

"That still doesn't mean –"

"I am not asking. We will make sure the company survives and you will be well provided for, but you must do your part."

"You mean go to prison for something I didn't do?." Rodrick slammed his brandy glass down on the table and stood. "I won't do it." He pointed his finger at Rolf. "This is your mess, you own up to it."

"You aren't without guilt, big brother. Shall I remind you of the millions you funneled off Moretti?"

"I didn't know he was a crime lord. You told me he was legitimate."

"Some of his interests are."

"But not all."

"No, not all." Robert agreed. "Nevertheless, as your brother stated, you are not without guilt. And Moretti poses as much of a threat to the family as the government. He's made his position clear. Return his investment – to the penny or he won't only help to shut us down, he'll eliminate us."

"Eliminate? As in kill?"

"That was I took from the conversation, yes."

"So how are you going to get him his money?"

"Dear boy, I am not. You are. You took it, you put it back."

"I don't have it!"

"Then who does?"

"Analise. Well, actually David. She took half of it and put it into a trust for him."

"Then I strongly suggest that your first course of action is to get it back."

"And then go to prison?."

"If it comes to that, yes. Come now, Rodrick. Should you go to prison, it's highly unlikely that you'd be there for more than a few years. And it's not as if you would be sent somewhere that hardened criminals such as murderers and terrorists are housed. For god's sakes, act like a man for once in your life."

Rodrick was dumbstruck. "Act like a man? How dare you? How dare either of you sit there and tell me you're going to frame me for the shit you got us into? What if I say no? What then?"

"The decision has been made. If anyone looks, the trail will lead to you. Denying it will serve no purpose. It's done. You will be amply rewarded."

"Fuck you." Rodrick couldn't believe what he was hearing. What made it worse was the smug smile on his brother's face. "Fuck both of you."

With that, he stormed out of the house and jumped in his car. The moment he did, he pulled out his phone and called Gina. "I need to see you. Now."

Seconds later he roared down the drive of the estate, headed for the city. His mind whirled with futy. He had to come up with a way to thwart his father's plan because there was no way in hell he was going to prison.

*****

Riley spotted Cody when he pulled up at the ranch house. She was standing outside the paddock, one booted foot on the bottom rail of the fence, leaning on the top rail. He climbed out of the truck and made his way across the uneven ground.

He hadn't seen Analise since the day she arrived in Cotton Creek. They had texted a few times and had spoken once on the phone, but things felt strained and uncomfortable. That kicked him in the gut. Damn if he didn't miss taking to her over the 'net.

Cody said Analise had been pretty upset at first because she felt that he'd deliberately misled her. She confided in him it probably had a lot to be with Analise being such a big Nate Bridges fan. It's hard for anyone to come face-to-face with their movie idol. Finding out that the idol and the friend are one and the same might just throw anyone for a loop.

He was fair-minded enough to agree. Friends he'd had before he became a star had faded pretty fast from his life when he became famous. Some of that blame was his. He just quit calling. But he'd lost a few friends just because he was famous and they suddenly didn't know how to be themselves around him. He'd not found a way to repair things back then and didn't know how to now.

Once again, Cody came to the rescue.

As it turned out, Analise was gung ho about learning everything there was to learn about ranching and had been shadowing Cody day in and day out. Whatever work there was to do, she volunteered to help. Cody said that surprisingly, Analise had a real way with animals.

She was learning to ride, and Cody had joked that maybe she was practicing too much because there were some evenings she could barely sit – or stand for that matter.

When she had called Riley early that morning to ask him to join them on an afternoon ride out to Cotton Creek near Rascal Flats and have an old-fashioned camp out, he had almost begged off. She reminded him that if he wanted to mend fences he was going to have to start somewhere, so he agreed.

"What's up, half-pint?" He said as he came up behind Cody.

"Check this shit." She pointed toward the interior of the paddock.

"Is that...?"

"Hell yeah. Can you believe it? Twostep freaking loves her."

Riley shook his head and watched. Analise was in the paddock with a bunch of carrots in one hand stroking Twostep's nose with the other. As he watched, she stopped rubbing the horse, and headed for the opposite side of the paddock, turning her back on Twostep.

The horse whinnied, pawed the ground once and whinnied again. She ignored him and kept walking. Twostep blew a breath, shook his head and followed. When he reached her, he bumped her in the back with his nose.

Analise turned and offered him a carrot. He munched it down as she petted him and then she stopped and walked away again. Twice more he followed and was rewarded. The third time there were no more carrots, but she rubbed his face and talked to him.

And then walked away. "Here's the real test." Cody said.

Riley didn't respond. They both knew that the chances of Twostep following her again were slim. Cody had tried the same thing and the dang horse just wasn't inclined to be sociable if there wasn't something in it for him.

"Well I'll be damned." The words were out before he could stop them.

Not only had the horse followed and not received a reward, but he was nuzzling Analise's neck like she was his best friend.

"I know. I swear to god she's a natural- born horse whisperer."

He scoffed at Cody's notion. "No way."

"As God is my witness. You just saw it. A couple of days ago the new mare got spooked by a corn snake and we couldn't get her out of her stall. Annie went in and talked to her and the mare just followed her out like a damn puppy. It's freaky, Riley. Freaky."

Riley turned his attention to Analise in the paddock. She petted Twostep some more and then turned and looked across the paddock. Riley could see the look of surprise on her face when she saw him.

She crossed the paddock with Twostep at her side and stopped at the fence. "Riley, what a surprise."

Riley cut his eyes at Cody. "She didn't tell you?"

"Tell me what?"

"He's joining us for camping."

Analise looked from Cody to Riley and he could see her unease. For a moment he wondered if she was going to beg off but then she smiled a weak smile. "Great. I – I didn't know what people eat for this kind of thing here, but I packed up some food that can be eaten cold and some things that can be cooked over a fire."

"Then let's get loaded up and head out."

This time her smile seemed more genuine. "Okay. I'll go get the food."

"Sounds like a plan." Riley opened the gate for her and watched until she was walked into the house before he turned to Cody. "What're you up to, half-pint?"

"Nothin'."

"Um hmmm." He followed her to the tack room and for the next little while they both focused on saddling their three horses and getting another ready to load up with the supplies.

"You need anything outta your truck?" Cody asked when they finished.

"Bedroll and jacket. You need anything from the house?

"Same."

"Take your mount and the pack horse and gimme the reins to the other two. I'll grab my stuff and meet you at the house."

She did just that and he led the horses to his truck. It took less than a minute to grab his jacket and an old bedroll from behind the seat of his truck and secure it behind one of the saddles. He then led the horses to the house.

Cody kicked open the screen door of the house, tossed two bedrolls onto the porch and then disappeared back inside. Riley secured the bedrolls. Just as he was finishing the door banged open again. Cody and Analise emerged, each with a sizable sack in their hands.

Riley couldn't help wondering what was in the sacks but he didn't ask. He just secured them to the pack animal and swung up into his saddle.

Cody cut him an evil eye when he grinned at the way Analise grimaced as she climbed into the saddle. He marveled that she even wanted to ride. He could remember what it was like to not have been in the saddle for a while. Getting back to it had cost him more than a few days of soreness.

For the first couple of miles no one said a word. Analise must have taken fifty pictures in that time and he couldn't help but be amused. For people who lived here there didn't seem to be much to see, but for her it had to seem alien. The landscape of West Texas could best be described as unforgiving. Some saw the harshness of it and others the beauty. He wondered which camp she fell into.

Analise didn't know which emotion to go with – excitement or anxiety. It was exciting to be out riding across the barren landscape, watching the sky and searching the horizon that stretched out in seeming endlessness.

Not to mention the sight of Riley, riding a few yards to her right and a bit ahead of her. He rode with such ease and smoothness, it made her feel clumsy and awkward in comparison. But then so did Cody. She rode like she'd been born in the saddle.

Analise took a few dozen pictures of them. She loved the quick smile Cody would cut her, or the way Cody would gaze into the distance when no one was watching and the look that came over her face. It was like she was part of the landscape, joined with the land. Her expression seemed to convey reverence and love.

Riley? God, how to even begin to describe Riley. The young handsome film star had matured into a man in his fifties whose expressions have the sense of someone who had found peace, to a man with some turmoil inside to a silly grin that could light up the entire state of Texas.

Whatever the years had taken from him, it had given back in spades. He was still a strikingly handsome man, one who had a timeless appeal she'd be willing to bet would last his whole life.

It still rattled her that he was Nate Bridges. 'Shit on a stick' as her dad was fond of saying. She'd been lusting after that man since his first film and here she was, riding alongside him on a horse named Apache. She chuckled to herself as she heard the words to the old song in her head. "I've been to the desert on a horse with no name."

"What's got you smiling, Ms. Annie?" Riley asked, alerting her to the fact that he was looking at her.

She wasn't quite ready to meet his eyes. "Just feels good to be here."

"Yeah, it does."

"It's not what I had pictured in my head."

"No?"

"No. I mean, yes. I looked at all kinds of pictures online, but it's different to see it in person. It's the feel of the air, the smells and sounds."

"Far cry from New York." Cody commented from the other side of Analise.

"Oh god yes."

"Never been there." Cody said.

"Ever wanted to go?"

"Not really." She looked around Analise at Riley. "He's been."

"Do you like it?" Analise turned her attention to him.

"It's okay. Bit too many people for my taste. Too much noise. Hard to hear yourself think."

"It can be."

"So did you live in one of those big high rise things?" Cody asked.

Analise wasn't keen on talking about herself and her life in New York, but she didn't want to ruin the moment of comradery between them. "No. We didn't live in the city."

"So where'd you live?"

"In a house."

"With a yard?"

"Yes, we had a yard."

"A big house?"

Analise wished Cody would stop asking questions but she couldn't say so. "Big enough I guess."

"You go to the city much?"

"Occasionally."

"Do you miss it."

"Not at all."

"Really?"

"Yes."

"Huh. So I guess you can take the girl outta the city."

"I guess so. Oh what's that?"

Riley looked in the direction she pointed. "That's Cotton Creek."

Analise smiled at him. "So the town was named after the creek or the creek after the town?"

"I don't really know. Cody?"

"Grandma says her grandma said the town was named after the creek."

"Well there you go. Straight from Grandma Sweet's mouth."

"Why Cotton?" Analise asked.

"Pardon?"

"Why name it Cotton Creek?"

"Cuz people grew a lot of cotton." Cody answered.

"And there's more than a few cotton mouths in some parts of the creek." Riley added.

"Cotton mouths?" Analise shuddered. If there was one kind of animal on earth she didn't like it was snakes.

"Don't worry. They're not bad up this way."

"Thank God."

Everyone fell silent for the remainder of the ride. When they arrived, everyone got to work setting up camp. By the time they were done, the sun was sinking into the horizon. Analise fished out a plastic bag from one of the sacks.

"Who's up for a cold beer?"

"You have cold beer?" Riley turned from his task of building a fire to look at her.

"Yeah. I wet some hand towels and wrapped them around beer and put them in the freezer this morning. It'll keep beer ice cold for a good long time."

"How many you got?" Cody asked.

"A twelve-pack."

"That ought to just about do it." Riley said and grinned. "Soon as I get this fire started, I'm ready."

Riley watched Analise as she worked. Funny, but at the moment she didn't seem much like a city girl. Had spending time with Cody made that much of an impact? Whatever the case, it was nice to see that tension gone from her posture and a smile on her face.

Dinner was a surprise. Along with her ingenious way of keeping beer cool, she'd packed sausage and hotdogs to cook on the fire, and had made a potato salad that rivaled Stella's. She'd also brought buns and even a plastic container of baked beans she heated on the fire in a skillet she placed on what she said was a cake cooling rack balanced between two rocks.

There was even dessert. S'mores. The flavor reminded him of childhood campouts and brought back a lot of good memories.. By the time they finished eating they were all stuffed. While Cody burned the paper plates they'd used to eat off of in the fire, Analise had washed the skillet with water from a gallon jug she'd brought.

They sat around for a while talking and pretty soon everyone was yawning. "Okay, I'm done." Cody announced. "It's my one night to sleep and that's what I'm gonna do. See ya'll in the morning."

She unrolled her bedroll, climbed in and was asleep in two minutes. Riley looked at her, grinned and then turned his attention to Analise. "You tired, Annie?"

"Yeah, a little."

"Then why don't we turn in?"

"Sounds good."

He waited until she'd spread her bedroll and then placed his close by. As he lay down he heard her soft voice. "Thanks for taking me camping."

"Thanks for letting me join. See you in the morning, Annie."

"Goodnight, Riley."

It took Riley a bit to get to sleep but finally he felt himself sinking. It seemed that he had just shut his eyes when he heard Analise. "Riley!" Her voice was a stage whisper, sharp but low. "Riley!"

He rolled over and could see her lying on her back, staring at him. "Annie?"

"There's something in my sleeping bag."

"What?"

"There's something in here with me."

"Where?"

"It's across my left leg, just above my boot."

"Can you tell what it is?"

"I'm not about to touch it but it feels like a snake."

Riley cursed softly and climbed out of his bedroll. He quietly went over to where Analise was laying still as death. Her face was covered in a sheen of sweat.

"Okay, let me take a look." Without touching he checked out her bedroll. It wasn't zipped which explained how the snake had gotten in.

"Annie listen to me. I want you to move your left leg real easy out from under the bedroll."

"I don't want to anger it."

"Me either, but we've got to get it out. So real slow, slide your foot out."

"What if it bites?"

"Don't worry, you'll be fine, I'm right here. Just trust me, okay?"

"Okay."

"All right." He looked around and grabbed one of the more sizeable rocks that lined the fire. It was warm but not too hot to hold. "Okay, now, Annie."

He watched, straining his eyes in the darkness. He could see movement in the bedroll but couldn't tell what it was from. "Is that you or the snake?"

"Both of us, I think. He's kinda wrapped around my boot from the feel of it."

"That's good. Even if he bites he can't bite through the boot. So keep moving your foot out."

"Okay. No wait. What are you going to do once it's out?"

"I'm gonna – I'm gonna kill it with this rock."

"You're going to beat me with a rock?"

"No, the snake."

"Well if it's on me aren't you going to hit me?"

Riley realized he hadn't thought it out well. "You have a better idea?"

"Not really."

"Then we stick with my plan."

"Okay, here goes."

Analise's boot and then her leg slid out from under the bedroll. Sure as shit, there was a big fat snake wrapped around her ankle. A big fat mad snake that struck the moment her foot was free of the covers. Riley didn't have time to hit it. Analise bolted to her feet like she'd been propelled from a canon and was hopping around, slinging her foot like a crazy person.

The snake must have gotten hung in her jeans because it was flopping all around but not coming loose.

"Get this thing off me!" Analise yelled as she continued to jump and kick.

"If you'd hold still for five seconds I'll try!"

"I am!"

"Annie be still!"

She stopped, balancing on her right foot and holding her left aloft. Riley looked at the snake. It was clamped on tight to her jeans, twisting and writhing its body up around her leg. He wasn't real keen on what he was about to do, but he had to act so he took a breath and grabbed the snake at the base of its head.

Two hard jerks and the snake was off her leg and in his hand. Two seconds later he threw it away from him as hard as he could. He turned to look at Analise and she took a step toward him. His feet carried him the rest of the way. He almost reached for her but stopped short.

So did she. They simply looked at one another and damn if he didn't feel like he was falling. Not physically, but into something he wasn't prepared for. The attraction he felt for her slammed into him. Had Cody not been there he might have made a move. Had he not wanted so desperately to deny that attraction he might have kissed her.

Still, the impact was potent. The only thing that saved him was her suddenly bursting into laughter. At first it shocked him, then the humor of the situation hit him and before he knew it he was laughing as well.

"What the hell are you doing?" Cody was sitting up staring at the both of them

Analise laughed harder which caused him to laugh harder. Cody just looked at them like they'd lost their minds. "Pipe down. Some people are trying to sleep."

They finally got it under control and Analise reached out and touched his arm. "Thanks for saving me."

"Anytime, Annie."

She smiled and looked at her bedroll. "Would you think me a coward if I said I don't relish the idea of getting back in that thing?"

"I think I can fix that." He spread out his bag, rolled hers up and fashioned a pillow to put on his. "If you don't mind sharing."

She looked at the bedroll and then at him. "Fair warning, I think I snore."

"Then that makes two of us."

"Okay, deal. Which side you want?"

"The right."

She gestured for him to go first and he lay down on his back. She lowered down beside him on her back and then rolled toward him. "Do you mind?"

In lieu of an answer, he stretched out his arm and she snuggled up against his side, placing her head on his shoulder. Riley wrapped his arm around her. "Night Annie."

"Night Riley."

Riley lay there for a long time, watching the stars, feeling her relax against him. It was a nice feeling and just before he drifted off, he wondered how it would feel to have this feeling every night.

Chapter Eight

Rodrick walked out onto the balcony as Gina entered the room. He was on the phone with his son, David and had no desire for David to find out about Gina. Nor did he have any desire for Gina to know of his conversation with David.

"Texas? What in the world is your mother doing in Texas?"

"Visiting a friend."

"And her car broke down?"

"Yeah."

"So what is she going to do?"

"Get it fixed, I guess."

"And what part of Texas did you say that was?"

"I didn't. Listen, Dad, I have to go. I'll talk to you later."

"All right. I love you, son."

"Yeah. Bye."

Rodrick stuck his phone in the breast pocket of his shirt, placed both hands on the balcony rail, and stared out over the city. David had been less than forthcoming about his mother. That wasn't a surprise. He'd always favored his mother. But Rodrick needed to know where she was so he could try to convince her to give back the money she'd taken.

The balcony door opened and Gina walked out. "Who was that on the phone?"

"My son."

"Oh? I didn't think you and he were speaking? He *is* still tied to her apron strings isn't he?"

Rodrick ignored the jibe. "I think I need to find Analise, speak with her in person. I'm sure I can convince her to give me back the money and then I can—"

Gina's laugh cut him short. "What?"

She waved her hand as if dismissing something ridiculous. "Darling, take it from someone who knows. She'll never give you back that money."

"You don't know that. If she thought I was in trouble – in danger—"

"You cheated on her, Ricky. She wouldn't spit on you if you were on fire. Besides, that little matter is already being handled."

A wave of fear brought bile boiling up his throat. "What do you mean by that?"

Again the dismissive hand wave. That was starting to annoy him. "Just that. She'll be dealt with, you'll pay what you owe and that will demonstrate your loyalty. After that it's just a matter of dealing with your family and when it's all said and done and you're in control of Becke Ltd, then you and I can live happily ever after."

She pinned him with a look sharp enough to cut. "That *is* what you want, isn't it?"

"You know it is, but I can't imagine how you could possibly— and what do you mean demonstrate my loyalty? To whom?"

Gina's smile seemed a bit sinister, something that surprised him. "Darling, I haven't been entirely honest with you."

"About what?"

"Well, about my – my family."

"What do you mean?"

"I mean – well, my name isn't really Russo. That's my mother's maiden name. My real name is Gina Moretti."

Rodrick literally had to hold onto the balcony railing to remain standing. "Moretti? As in Giancarlo Moretti?"

She nodded. "My daddy."

Rodrick felt like he was going to vomit. He turned away from her, feeling sweat bead on his forehead and gather under his arms. Giancarlo Moretti was the head of the largest crime syndicate in New York, and one of the people to whom his family owed millions.

He tried to gather his wits before he turned his head to look at her. "And you're telling me this now because?"

"Because I love you. I want to spend my life with you, Ricky. And my father has the power to eliminate all your problems."

"In exchange for what?"

"Can't he just do it because he loves me and wants me to be happy?"

"But he won't, will he? What does he want from me?"

"Nothing that you haven't already been doing. He just wants you at the head of the table of Becke Ltd."

"And what about my family? My father and brother?"

"They're not really necessary."

"Gina, they're setting me up. If the Feds come in, Rolf has made sure it will be my name on everything underhanded and illegal. I told you, they expect me to take the fall."

"No. Daddy won't let that happen. He has power. Real power. Just think about it, Ricky. We will be like kings of our own empire. He can make that happen, Ricky. With my father's help, you'll make more than you ever imagined and we can have the life we've dreamed of. All we have to do it get rid of what stands in our way."

"Like my family."

She shrugged. "Attaining greatness always requires a sacrifice. Attaining me does as well. You do want me, don't you?"

"You know I do. I told you a million times. I love you, Gina. I've never loved anyone the way I love you."

"Then all you have to do is prove it, lover. We'll take care of your wife and when you pay my father and demonstrate your loyalty, he'll take care of the rest of it."

Rodrick shook his head. "He can't take care of the federal investigation, Gina."

"Maybe not. But like I said he can make sure that all the evidence points to your brothers and your father. You were the innocent in all this, the honorable son and brother who was duped. No one will be able to touch you."

Rodrick was shocked that her plan had appeal. On one hand, it was like being offered a 'get out of jail free' card, a chance to be the man in charge, to rule the empire with Gina by his side. On the other hand it meant becoming something he was not. A man willing to murder to get what he wanted.

He didn't know what to do. If he said no, he would lose Gina, and possibly his life. If Moretti was willing to kill Rodrick's entire family, then killing him would not even cause the man to bat an eye.

He was fucked and his options were dismal. He could say no and risk being killed, or go to prison with the rest of his family if they were indicted. Or he could say yes and become a monster like Moretti. He really didn't like either option. But he was going to have to choose one and he was going to have to do it fast, because Gina was a woman accustomed to getting what she wanted, without having to wait.

"Gina, you know I'd do anything for you." It was the best he could manage at the moment, and he was relieved when she apparently took it as acquiescence. She came to him winding her arms around him.

"You won't be sorry, Ricky. I promise you."

God help him, but even fear at discovering that she was spawned by a monster and was most likely one herself, could not stop him from becoming aroused. He let her lead him into the penthouse, down the hall and to the bedroom.

He didn't think sex was going to ease his mind, but it would keep her from being suspicious that he wasn't onboard. He needed to keep her believing that he would do what she wanted. At least until he figured out what path provided the best options for survival.

*****

Analise looked at herself in the mirror. "I'm not sure about this."

"Oh come on, you look great."

She turned to look at Cody. "It's … it's too young for me don't you think?"

"For crying out loud, Annie. You're not a freaking grandma. You look great. And besides, people around here wear jeans and shirts when they're a hundred."

Analise gave herself another look then threw up her hands. "Fine, but if I get laughed out of town it's on your head."

"No danger out that. Riley's gonna—"

"Don't. Please."

"Look, I know you have a fantasy thing about who he was in the movies and all, and yeah, he was smokin' hot back in the day, but now he's just Riley. I mean, don't get me wrong, he's still smokin' hot for an old guy, but he's not the movie star. And he's never acted like one. Around here, he's just Riley Morgan."

"Smokin' hot Riley Morgan."

"A bit old for my taste, but yeah.. And you're smoking hot Annie Becke so get over it. And I gotta get to the bar and get things set up. What time you want me to come get you?"

"I don't know. You tell me."

"Between five and six? I'll get Hannah to watch the bar."

"Cody if this is going to be an inconvenience, I can just stay here."

"Hell no, you can't. You haven't stepped foot off this ranch since you got here except to go camping. This is the big night, girl and you are gonna be there. I'll call when I'm on my way."

"Okay, and thank you."

"No need."

"Is there anything I can do while you're gone? Clean or ... or whatever?"

"Whatever you want. Me casa and all that. Later!"

Analise watched Cody leave and then looked at herself in the mirror again. She'd never worn jeans this low cut or tight in her life and felt like an idiot. She quickly changed back into her comfortable loose- fit jeans and t-shirt and went downstairs.

She wandered into the kitchen. The dishes from breakfast were still in the sink. It took less than ten minutes to wash, dry and put things where they belonged. As she did, she noticed again that nearly all of the cupboards were in disarray. Until now she'd been hesitant to do anything without asking. But those cupboards were in need of serious work.

Before she'd given it a thought she was busy unloading everything, washing down the inside of the cupboards and placing everything back in a nice orderly fashion. She hummed to herself as she worked, letting her mind wander.

It was nice being able to admit to someone that knowing Riley was Nate Bridges had really thrown her for a loop. As unlikely a pair as they were, she and Cody really had formed a connection and she knew through and through she could trust Cody.

Even now she got a rush of heat to her skin when she thought about Riley. Holy shit, she was going to have to set aside an entire afternoon to tell Katie about this. Never in a million years would she have imagined it. It was simply unbelievable that she'd made online friends with someone and then to have him turn out to be the actor she'd been lusting over the last twenty years.

Now not only had she met him in person, they camped together and he'd rescued her from a snake and she had even slept snuggled up next to him. It was like something out of a book.

Sometimes life was stranger than fiction. And that made her remember. She needed to enter the notes she'd jotted down earlier on paper into the computer. Thanks to Amazon, she'd been able to get a cool tablet pc in just a few days, and they'd shipped it right to Cody's door.

She finished the kitchen and headed for the den where she'd left the tablet on a small wooden desk. She turned it on, opened Word and got to work.

Riley turned into the road leading to the Sweet Ranch and slowed. He hadn't seen Analise since the campout. That was cowardice on his part. He hadn't wanted to face her one-on-one. On the one hand, he didn't feel that he'd done anything wrong, acted dishonorably or even actually lied to her.

On the other, they had not addressed the issue of him being Nate Bridges and sooner or later they had to if their friendship was going to get fully back on track. He could understand how she'd think he'd been trying to keep his alter ego a secret. And truth be told, he had been on some level. Despite being out of show business for a decade, if he told someone he was Nate Bridges, they always treated him differently. People were uncomfortable around celebrities. They saw themselves as less than the celebrity, even though that was a big crock of crap.

Still, it was hard to make friends with "stardom" in the way. And he'd been out of the game so long that he didn't think of himself as Nate anymore. Hell, he never wanted to be that man again.

But there was more at play than his discomfort at keeping his Nate persona a secret. Meeting Analise in person had kind of knocked him off kilter. Had she been a homely woman, or a woman he'd never be attracted to in a million years it would have been easier.

He'd come to know her fairly well over the last year. Gotten to know what made her laugh, what made her angry and what made her sad. He knew her fierce devotion to her son and how hurt, let-down and angry her husband's infidelity had made her.

Riley admired her. She was strong-willed, talented and had a good heart. He liked her, genuinely enjoyed her company. He'd just never expected to be attracted to her. He'd thought the picture of her was pretty, but in person she was really something. Long dark hair that had a few strands of gray she obviously didn't try to hide with dye, clear baby-blue eyes rimmed with dark long lashes and a skin that was clear and smooth, not hidden under layers of artifice.

Then there was her body. His first impression was "pin-up" – that kind of woman that makes a man's mouth water. Big breasts, full hips and that sultry full-lipped look that had always drawn him like a horse to water.

That's what had thrown him so hard. It was one thing to like a woman, admire her and enjoy talking – or in their case, texting with her. But to be that attracted added a whole new level to things. And the truth was, Riley didn't know if he was ready for the way she riled him up inside. It wasn't like she was the kind of woman he could take to his bed and then never speak to again. Unfortunately his relationships during the last decade had been of that sort.

He'd hadn't planned driving out to the Sweet ranch today. But he'd driven into town to stock the kitchen and while there stopped by to see Jimmy to ask about Analise's RV. Jimmy mentioned that there was a lot of stuff still in it and he didn't want anything to go missing. He asked Riley to get her stuff and take it to her.

Riley's plan was to put everything in his truck and take it to the bar. That way Cody could take it to the ranch where Analise was staying. He would have done just that if he had not seen the treasure box she'd been working on.

He was downright shocked. It might have been something she purchased unfinished, one of those cookie-cutter chests you can buy about anywhere, but she'd turned it into something special. It was clear that she'd not only listened to what he'd told her, but had done one hell of a job and added her own touches to boot.

The finish looked to be a mix of stain colors that had resulted in a honey tone with some rust overtones that gave it a slightly aged look. She'd let the stain build up in the crevices of the carvings on the top to make them stand out, and she'd somehow gotten a pattern created along the edges so that it appeared to have an inlaid border.

He was not only impressed, but curious as to how she'd done it. Riley knew the kind of time it took to create something that beautiful. It was sanded smooth as glass and had a polished rather than sealed look, which spoke to him of many hours of oiling and buffing. He knew the care and love that went into something like this, and that spoke volumes to him.

God help him but that that wooden chest did it. It didn't matter what the women in his past had done to hurt him. She wasn't them. She was Annie. His Annie. The woman who was trying to rebuild her life with the same care and focus as she built this chest. He had to take it to her. Had to see her and try and make things right between them. Whatever right was.

He coasted to a stop in front of the house and sat there staring while trying to figure out what he was going to say. The front door opened and Analise stepped out onto the porch. She didn't smile or wave, just stood there watching, her hands crammed in the pockets of her jeans.

Riley climbed out of the truck and reached over the side, into the bed to lift out the chest. When he turned toward the house, Analise's hands had moved. The fingers of both hands now covered her mouth.

He walked to the house and up the steps, his eyes on her. He could see the glistening in her eyes and once he was on the porch looking down at her, knew that glistening was tears that had gathered and were threatening to spill over.

"I knew you'd want this. You did a real fine job on this, Annie."

"Thank you, Riley."

"So I'm fully back to Riley?"

"My friend Riley saved me from a snake. And only my friend Riley would know how important this is to me. Nate Bridges wouldn't."

"Then can I come in? I don't know what you got in here, but it's getting a might heavy."

She smiled, brushed at the tears and opened the door for him.

"Where you want me to put this?"

105

"Could you put it on the kitchen table for now?"

"Yep."

He walked into the kitchen and stopped short. His stop must have been more abrupt than he realized because she ran right into the back of him.

"Oh sorry. What's wrong?"

"What happened?" Riley had been in Cody's house a lot of times and not once had he ever seen the kitchen this clean.

"What do you mean?"

"It's clean."

"Oh," she laughed and pushed at him. "I didn't have anything to do so I cleaned."

Riley set the chest on the table and ran his hand over it. "You did a hell of a job on this Annie."

"Why have you called me Annie since I got here? You never did before."

He turned to face her and for a moment they were both frozen, gazes locked. "Analise is the woman who lived in New York. She wouldn't take off across the country in an RV all by herself. Annie – well, Annie's the woman who would. She'd drive all the way to Texas to meet a friend and she'd create something as beautiful as this chest, putting in the hours, giving it the time and love it deserved so its beauty could be revealed."

Analise had never heard anything as wonderful or beautiful as those words. She couldn't stop the tears that spilled down her cheeks.

"Damn, Annie. I didn't mean to make you cry."

She shook her head and laughed through the tears. "I think that's the nicest thing anyone has said to me in … in a very long time. Thank you."

Riley reached over to cup the side of her face with his hand, his thumb brushing away the last of the tears. Once more their gazes locked and they were frozen in place. Annie could barely breathe. The touch of his hand evoked emotions and reactions that were almost overwhelming. His eyes held something – some emotion that held her spellbound.

Finally he smiled. "Just sayin' it like it is. Now, about this chest…"

His hand moved away and he turned to the chest. "How did you create this border? It looks like a wood inlay."

"Oh!" Analise mentally shook herself, trying to regain mental composure. She opened the chest and took out a case. "This." It was a Dremel tool. "I used a metal ruler as a guide and carved the little depression and then created the pattern. If you go really easy it makes it look kind of like little chunks of wood that have been glued down."

"And the colors?"

"I bought different stains and painted it with a little brush and then I put a finish coat of the tung oil and didn't buff it and it made it really shiny."

Riley leaned over, placing his hands on the table to study the chest. "This is really fine work, Analise."

107

"Annie." She said quietly and when he looked at her in surprise, she smiled. "Please, I think I like that better."

"Well, so do I. And I'm really impressed, Annie. In fact, I'm working on a piece for Stella and Billy – Cody's parents. Billy took a spill a few weeks back and kind of demolished a side table they had in their living room that was from Stella's folks. He wanted to make it up to her so I'm making a replacement. I'm not too good on the intricate stuff, but I have some pictures so maybe you could help me with me."

"I'd love to." She was thrilled that he would ask.

"Yeah?"

"Yes."

"Well good. Maybe I could come by tomorrow morning and take you over to my place. I'd planned on working on it tomorrow."

"Aren't you going to the festival tomorrow?"

"Naw. I'll be there tonight and that'll be enough for me. But if you'd rather go to—"

"No, I wouldn't. I'd love to come help you in your shop. I've been so curious about it; I'm dying to see it."

"It's not much to see."

"It is to me."

"Well good then, it's a date."

A date? She had a date with Riley? She felt a flutter of excitement. "Yes it is."

Her phone rang and she looked pulled it from her back pocket. "It's Cody."

"Go ahead."

She gave him a smile and answered. "Hey Cody. I was just talking with Riley…. Yes, he brought some of my things from the RV. I hope you don't mind. Oh! Ok, hold on and I'll ask."

She moved the phone slightly away from her face and looked at Riley. "Cody wants to know if it'd be too much trouble for you to give me a ride to the bar. Hannah is going to be late and Billy is busy with the pig so it's going to be a while before she can come get me."

"Be happy to."

"Thanks." She smiled and lifted the phone back to her ear. "He will. Thanks, Cody. See you later."

She put the phone down on the table and looked at Riley. "So what time do you want to go?"

"Around six?"

"Works for me."

"Oh, I almost forgot. Jimmy said he made some calls and he thinks he can fix your rig but it will take three to four weeks more to get the parts."

"That long?"

"Is that long?"

"Well, it is when you're imposing on someone. I don't know if Cody will want me around that long."

"If you keep her kitchen this clean she will. And between you and me, since you can cook that's a bonus. That girl can burn water."

Analise chuckled. "Then I guess I'll just have to ask her."

"Well, if she says no and you can cook, I'll put you up."

"Really?"

"It's the least a friend can do."

Riley saw the surprise and something else register on Annie's face and for the third time since he'd walked into the house, their eyes locked. Damn if there wasn't something enticing there, the way her eyes darkened a bit and the slight flush that bloomed on her cheeks.

It inspired thoughts he'd not had in a while. Sure there were lascivious thoughts, but Annie inspired imaginings of long walks at sunset, slow dances and kisses that could make a man lose track of time. It shocked him and it made him a bit nervous. Nervous enough that he moved away, went to the refrigerator and pulled out a pitcher of tea

"So, what does your family think about you being stranded in Cotton Creek?" He searched the cupboards for a glass.

"David thought the whole thing was hilarious and told me I should use it in a book."

Riley took his glass back to the refrigerator and opened up the freezer section at the top. There was a pail of ice inside. He filled his glass and then looked at Annie. "Want me to fix you a glass?"

"No thanks. I've had enough coffee today that my caffeine quota is way over the line."

Riley chuckled. "So, your son is okay with you being here?" He filled his glass with tea and made another trip back to the refrigerator to put the pitcher away.

"Yes."

"What about your husband?"

There was dead silence. Riley turned to look at her. "Annie?"

She just stood there, smile gone from her face and her stance one of tension.

"You okay, Annie?"

She nodded and looked away for a moment. "I…I didn't tell you everything about my leaving New York."

"Oh?"

"I left for good. Left him."

Riley leaned back against the counter. "I know you'd had some …some trouble."

"Oh, like him cheating on me for the last three years with some woman young enough to be his daughter, and his family being investigated for fraud and money laundering and him threatening to burn the house down with me in it? Yeah, we've had some trouble."

Riley was shocked. He knew Annie had not been all that happy and that she'd mentioned she was thinking of leaving but he figured it was just a couple going through a rough patch. "Investigated?"

She nodded again. "I think he's going to prison, Riley. And even if he doesn't, I can't see the point in staying. He doesn't love me. He's in love with that girl. And oddly, that doesn't even hurt because I realized that I don't love him either."

As she spoke she realized that her words weren't empty. Whatever hurt Rick had given with his infidelity had faded. She'd lost her love for him long before now.

111

"The man I married disappeared a long time ago. He went into business with his family and became someone I didn't know and didn't really want to. I stayed for David, but he's grown now, all moved into an apartment in Cambridge and excited about his life.

"There's nothing left for me there. So, I left him."

"And bought an RV and toured the country."

That brought the ghost of a smile to her face. "Yes. And came to Texas. I got to see my friend Katie, and make a new friend in Cody and I got to meet you. And that makes it worth it."

"So, I guess if you're not planning on going back it doesn't much matter how long it takes to fix your rig."

"You're absolutely right." This time the smile that formed on her face was full blown. "I'm free to do what I want. And right now there's nowhere else I'd rather be."

That tore it. Annie was not married. Well, she was, but she'd left her cheating husband so she was a free woman. Riley couldn't handle what ripped through him. He and Annie were friends and no friends should be thinking what he was thinking at the moment. She was free and all he wanted was to get his hands on her.

"Then let's get the rest of your stuff out of the truck."

"Okay."

Together they went out to his truck. There wasn't all that much, but it took two trips. They piled everything in the front room. "I think I should call Cody and ask her about staying before I haul this to the room that she let me use."

"Okay. I need to get back home, and take care of a couple of things. Be back at six."

"All right. I'll be ready."

She walked him to the front porch and when he turned to face her, she reached out and gave his arm a gentle squeeze. "I'm glad you came over, Riley. I was really nervous about seeing you."

"Oh, because of the –"

"Yes, the movie star thing. You're always going to be that, you know. It's part of who you are, but I'm glad I can see you for you – for Riley, I mean. And if you don't mind me saying so, I think he just might be every bit as special as Nate."

Riley was in motion before he could stop himself. His hand reached out to cup her face. "Annie."

"Yes?" Her eyes searched his and what he saw in them slayed him. If he didn't leave now he was going to make a huge mistake.

"That's the nicest thing I've heard in a long time. Thank you."

"What are friends for?" Her voice was just above a whisper.

"Amen to that." He moved away. "See you at six."

"I'll be waiting."

Riley made it to his truck and blew out his breath. What in the world was happening here? He wasn't prepared for the feelings Annie Becke inspired, and didn't want to do anything to ruin their friendship.

But at this point he wasn't sure he was going to be able to be around her and keep his hands off her.

"Yep, you're screwed, brother," he said to his reflection in the rear view mirror. "Totally screwed."

Chapter Nine

Analise was ready twenty minutes early. She'd spoken with Cody about the amount of time it was going to take to repair her RV and Cody invited her to stay as long as she wanted. Analise was very grateful, and had put all of her belongings into the room she was using and then had cleaned the entire house.

Everything was 'spic and span' as her mother used to say, right down to the windows. Even with doing that, she was still ready twenty minutes early and sitting perched on the edge of the couch, waiting for Riley.

She thought about calling Katie, but twenty minutes would not be enough time to tell her everything. Besides, Katie had been a bit freaked out since Analise was at her house. The last night Analise was there someone threw a rock through the front glass door of Katie's house.

Naturally, Katie had called the police and they chalked it up to juvenile vandalism, but Katie didn't feel safe staying in the house until the door was repaired. Analise helped her go to the local Home Depot and get a piece of plywood cut to cover the door. They had to buy a hammer and nails but they got the door covered.

And then Katie decided to go and stay with her sister who lived an hour away. Just until the door was properly repaired. She invited Analise, but that didn't seem right. Analise had never met Katie's sister and didn't want to impose. She thanked Katie and they said their goodbyes. Analise had found a campground to stay for the night.

Since then, she and Katie had not really communicated much. Analise had let her know she'd arrived in Cotton

Creek but had said nothing else about the RV breaking down or meeting Riley.

Meeting Riley. God, what a shock. Even now she could barely believe it. Nate Bridges was her all-time favorite heart throb. She'd watched his films so many times she could recite the lines. And she'd been one of those fans who would pick up a tabloid in the grocery store just because his photo was on the cover.

To meet him in person and have him turn out to be Riley had knocked her for a real loop. Thankfully their time together at the camping trip and then again earlier in the day had reminded her who he was – at least who he was now. She'd liked him for a year and had secretly wished that he could be some handsome cowboy that one day she would meet and maybe sparks would fly.

That was primarily due to how nice he was, and his ability to laugh at things and make her laugh as well. Theirs was an odd friendship, she supposed. Conducted online, or via text with never even hearing the other's voice or knowing how the other looked.

And yet, she'd become attached to him. Enough to drive to Cotton Creek just to meet him.

She leaned back and closed her eyes, remembering the shock of seeing him for the first time, and then the feelings he evoked in her today when his eyes met hers and then when he touched her. It had been a long time since a man had touched her in any way, much less as something that gentle. And it had unhinged her.

Now she'd be lucky to ever stop fantasizing about him.

The sound of an engine had her opening her eyes and getting up to go to the front door. She could see him coming up the drive, a rooster tail of dust in the wake of his truck. He pulled to a stop in front of the house and got out. She pulled the front door closed behind her and headed in his direction.

This was his day for surprises. If he'd thought he was attracted to Annie before, then he hadn't known the half of it. She was dressed in a pair of snug jeans that rode low on her hips with a long-sleeved knit top that clung to her body like a second skin. Worn boots peeked out from the hem of the jeans. It might not have affected another man in the same way, but to him, at that moment she was the sexiest thing he'd ever laid eyes on.

They met halfway and stopped. "Well hey there, cowgirl."

Annie laughed. "Hey yourself. You sure clean up nice, Riley Morgan."

Riley was surprised. "Where the hell did that accent come from Ms. New York?"

"Georgia."

"Okay, I want to hear more, but first, you ready to ride?"

"That I am."

"Well, let's go."

They got into his truck and he turned around and headed back down the drive. "So, Georgia?"

"It's where I grew up."

"What part?"

"The mountains. Cleveland area near Wildcat Mountain. My family owns a campground there."

"Wildcat Mountain? Well cut me off and call me shorty. And here I thought you were a big city girl."

"Not really. I got a scholarship and moved to New York to go to college and … well you know the rest of it."

"So did you stop and visit your folks on the way down?"

"No."

"Mind if I ask why?"

"Not quite ready for them to say I told you so."

Riley nodded. "I take it they're not a fan of the husband?"

"Ex-husband. And no. They're not."

"But they're still your folks."

"Yes, and I love them. I'm just not ready for them to know what's happened. Not until I'm settled and can assure them that everything is fine. And I took a step toward that today."

"What kind of step?"

"I hired a lawyer to file for divorce."

"That's a big step, Annie. You sure you want to do that?"

"One hundred percent." She turned and looked him dead in the eyes.

"Then good for you."

"And another cause for celebration."

"You have more than one?"

"Yes. I'm going to my first annual Cotton Creek barbecue festival. I get to hear one of my best friends sing with his band, I'm going to see my other new friend, Cody and meet her family in a less dramatic manner. I'm gonna drink some beer, eat some pig, meet some new people and if I'm real lucky some handsome cowboy will ask me to dance. So I'm going to enjoy this night and try to remember every moment so I can call my friend Katie tomorrow and tell her all about it."

"Well that sounds like a good time just waitin' to happen."

"Damn Skippy."

Riley burst out laughed and she reached over and pinched his arm. "What's so funny?."

"Just …I just had this mental image of you in my head. This writer with an imagination as big as the ocean, more curious than a bag of cats – someone who loved to laugh and wasn't afraid to get her hands a little dirty but also of a big city gal, all slick and polished. And…" He cut his eyes at her. "In some ways you're just what I thought and in others not at all."

She was silent and when he looked at her she had turned to look out of the window. "Annie? You okay?"

"Yeah. I was just wondering. Are you disappointed?"

"About what?"

"About me. Who I am."

Riley reached over and gave her a squeeze right above the knee. "Not a bit, Wildcat girl."

She smiled at him and he was so caught up in looking at her that he almost ran off the road and might have done just that if she hadn't alerted him with a "watch out there Turbo, I'd like to make it to the party in one piece."

"Yes, ma'am." Riley grinned. Not only was Annie a woman who turned him into the equivalent of a horny teenager, she was a friend that he genuinely liked being around. Maybe he should take a page from her book and stop analyzing and worrying and just enjoy the moment.

When they arrived, the parking lot was packed, people tailgating, eating, drinking, talking and laughing. Voices called out greetings as they made their way to the bar. Riley had hold of Annie's hand, leading the way and had no doubt that by morning the gossip would be all over town about him and the 'city woman' who came to visit and broke down in the middle of town.

Hell, there was already talk according to Cody. More than one rendition of him carrying Annie to the Sweets had been told. But that was the way of small towns. They stepped inside the bar and two seconds later a voice boomed out.

"Well, it's about damn time."

Cody rounded the bar to them. "Damn if ya'll don't look good together."

Riley tensed. Cody was going to make Annie uncomfortable with talk like that, and if he was honest, it made him a little uncomfortable.

"Don't we just?" Annie replied sassily, surprising him enough that he looked down at her.

"Don't get your boxers in a bunch cowboy. God that smell is divine. I'm starving. Lead me to the food."

Cody laughed and grabbed Annie's hand. "Stick with me."

*****

Annie smiled over her shoulder at Riley as she let Cody pull her through the crowd. Cody led her to a big table where a handsome couple sat. Annie recognized the woman as Mrs. Sweet and the gorgeous blonde woman next to them as Hannah.

"Hey ya'll, this here is Riley's friend Annie. Annie you might remember my mom, Stella and my sister, Hannah."

"Yes, nice to meet you under less embarrassing circumstances."

Stella smiled sweetly. "It's a pleasure, Annie. I hope you and Riley will join us?"

Annie looked at Riley and he grinned. "You know it."

They took a seat. Riley beside the man and Annie between him and Hannah. "Oh, and this is my dad, Billy Sweet." Cody said. "And my little sister KC."

KC was as lovely as her sisters. She looked to be around sixteen and had a bright friendly smile.

"It's such a pleasure to meet you." Annie said to Billy and then looked at KC. "All of you."

She looked around at everyone. "I feel that I should know you all, I've heard so many wonderful things about you from Riley."

"Been talking about us, eh?" Billy asked with a smile.

"Billy don't pick." Stella scolded in a teasing tone.

"I'm gonna go get the food." Cody announced. "Hannah, you wanna help?"

"Sure."

"I'll help." Analise offered. She was more comfortable with Cody around. Sitting at the table without her didn't have as much appeal.

"Oh you don't have to do that." Stella protested.

"But I want to. Hannah, you sit. I'll go help."

With that she got up and followed Cody into the back. The kitchen was bigger than she'd imagined and well laid out. There were five people fixing plates. Two men and three women. "Ya'll got my order up?" Cody asked the moment they walked in.

"Your arms broke?" One of the men, a young lanky guy with ginger hair asked with a grin.

Cody flipped him off with an answering grin and walked to the sink. Annie followed, washed her hands and after watching Cody, started filling plates in the same manner.

"Who's the new girl?" One of the women asked.

"My friend Annie. She's visiting. Annie, that's Mandy. And the blonde there is Sue Ellen. That sassy mouth is Mickey and the dude over there is Herbie. Everyone this is Annie. She's a Yankee but don't hold that against her, and be nice Mickey"

"I'm always nice."

Cody snorted and got to work.

"So you're from New York?" Mickey asked.

"Well, I lived there for twenty years."

"So where were you before that?" he asked.

"Born and raised in Georgia. In the mountains."

"A real Georgia peach eh?" Cody teased.

Analise laughed. Between answering questions on what she was doing in Cotton Creek and how long she was going to be there, Annie put together three plates. Cody passed her a big serving tray, loaded her own and started back to the table.

Annie thanked her brief stint as a waitress in college as she maneuvered through the people to the Sweet's table.

"You look like you know what you're doing there, Annie." Billy grinned at her as she put a plate down in front of Hannah and KC and then one at her own place.

"I'm not a stranger to waitressing, if that's what you mean." Annie looked around for a place to put the serving tray and smiled at Cody as she took it.

"So sit. Sit and eat." Stella urged.

Annie took her seat and Riley poured her a mug of beer from the pitcher in the center of the table. "To family and friends, old and new." He said after her glass was full and he'd lifted his own.

"Amen to that, brother." Billy echoed the sentiment and everyone toasted.

Then they all dug in. One bite of the barbecue had Analise groaning in appreciation. "Oh my god, this is good. That's the best barbecue sauce I ever tasted. Not the tang of the Memphis style and not the heavy brown sugar of the Georgia sweet but ... god that's good."

"Billy's secret recipe." Riley said in a loud stage whisper.

"And a damn good one. My hat's off to you, Mr. Sweet."

"Billy."

Analise smiled her thanks and then her attention was taken by KC who had a million questions about New York, and Hannah who wanted to know about the shopping and the fancy restaurants and even Stella who asked about the bakeries there.

The meal passed with laughs and good food and quite a bit of beer. They were just finishing up when a loud crash from the bar had Billy and Cody both getting to their feet. "I've got it, Dad." She raced off.

A few minutes later she returned. "Dang Tommy. He let the tap run over and Jenny slipped on it and busted her head. Doc and Dale are taking her over to Doc's to stitch her up . Doc says it might not even need stitches but he wants to keep an eye on her for a while. That puts us a server short. Hannah you think you can—"

"I'll do it." Annie piped up. The way she saw it, it would give her a chance to talk to people and learn a little more about them and about Cotton Creek.

"Annie I can't ask—"

"You didn't. I volunteered. So tell me what to do."

"You sure?"

"Positive."

"Annie, honey, that's sweet as all get out, but we can't ask you to do that." Billy chimed in.

"I'd really like to, Billy. Where I come from isn't so different from here, I suspect and there we always help out a friend. So, please, let me help."

"Well, when you put it that way, we'd appreciate it, Annie."

She gave him a smile then stood and turned toward Cody. "Okay Boss, point me in the right direction."

After that, things were kind of a whirl for her. She took and delivered orders, refilled soft drink and beer pitchers and talked to what seemed like hundreds of people. She met the guys in the band with Riley, the local barber and the man who owned the feed store. She talked with the manager of the bank and his wife, and learned about their two teenaged kids and the one they had in college.

Annie got introduced to the woman who owned the local salon, or beauty shop as she called it, and the people who owned the hardware store, the grocery and the gas station. She even met a few guys who were roustabouts, and some hands from the different ranches.

What struck her was that down to a person, they all seemed to be good, hard-working people who were friendly and nice. Curious, as well. She answered her share of questions through the evening. By nine o'clock, her feet were starting to hurt and her arms were tired. She noticed the men setting up on the stage and as she watched, Riley turned, looked at her and smiled.

That moment froze her in place. Standing there with a laden tray from bussing a table in one hand and two empty pitchers in the other, she felt like Cinderella at the ball when the handsome prince noticed her. All she could do was stand there and look back at him, seeing the slow smile that rose on his face and the way his eyes never left hers. It hit her like the proverbial freight train. She was dangerously close to falling for Riley Morgan.

The realization nearly staggered her and she felt the smile slide away from her face. She saw his expression change as well. His smile faded but his eyes never left hers. Annie had no clue how long they stood there, gazes locked.

All she knew was that suddenly Cody was slapping her on the shoulder.

"Okay, time for a break, girl."

Annie jerked her head to look at Cody. "Huh?"

"Oh boy." Cody gave a low whistle.

"What?"

"Nothing. Get rid of that stuff, grab a beer and take a load off. Dad said to come over and sit with Mama and KC. The band's gonna start up any minute."

"I can still help."

"You've done more than your share Annie and I appreciate it, but we're good. No one much will be eating from here on in and Hannah and I can handle the bar. Besides you've never heard Riley sing."

"Is he as good as I think? That video you sent was nice but there was a lot of noise."

"Oh yeah, he's good. Now scoot. Hannah has you a beer waiting at the bar."

Annie did as instructed, delivered the tray and pitchers to the kitchen and then went to the bar. "Here ya go, hon." Hannah slid a big mug her way. "We sure do appreciate you helping out, Annie."

"It was the least I could do. Cody's been so nice to me and you and your mama were so kind when I got here and – well you know."

"Actually I don't. All I know is Riley marched in the house like some hero out of a novel, with you unconscious in his arms. It was kind of romantic, to be honest. I thought you and he were – you know."

"Oh! Oh no. We're just friends. That was actually the first time I ever saw him in person. Heck, at all. I had no idea he was – you know, famous."

"Oh yeah, Nate Bridges. He was something back in the day wasn't he?" Hannah's gaze moved toward the stage.

"He still is." Annie murmured and then turned to Hannah. "How much for the beer?"

"On the house, hon. And as many more as you want."

"Thanks, Hannah. I think I'm going to go sit and enjoy the show."

"Okay. Have fun."

Annie made her way to Stella Sweet's table. "Mind if I sit with you?"

"Not at all, honey."

Annie took a seat and looked at the stage. "So Billy is a musician, too?"

Stella smiled. "Oh yes, Billy loves his music."

"And so do you, I'm guessing?"

Stella chuckled. "I surely do."

Annie turned her attention back to the stage. Billy and Riley stepped up to the microphone and Riley spoke. "Hey, ya'll. First of all, a big round of applause for Billy and all the fine folks here at Billy's. That was some mighty fine barbecue."

Everyone clapped, cheered, stomped their feet and hooted and Annie joined in. When the noise died, Riley looked over at Billy and Billy leaned in to speak into the microphone. "Since it's my bar, we're gonna start out with a little something for the most beautiful, kind-hearted and perfect woman in the world, my beautiful wife. Stella Mae, this one's for you, honey."

The crowd went wild cheering and hollering and Annie added her voice to the mix, watching the way Stella smiled at Billy. The band kicked off, Billy and Riley singing harmony to a song the country singer Randy Travis made famous – 'Forever and Ever, Amen'.

When they got to the chorus, the entire bar joined in. At first Annie just watched but by the second chorus she sang right along with everyone. When the song ended she clapped and cheered and was thinking what a wonderful time she was having. She couldn't wait to tell Katie about it.

The band played five or six songs and then Riley spoke into the microphone. "Okay, folks. We're gonna do one more and then take a break and put some quarters in that juke box so you people can get to dancing. This last one is an old one, but one of my favorites."

When he started singing "I'm so lonesome I could cry", Annie darn near did. The room erupted at first with cheers and yells and then fell completely silent. Riley's voice filled the bar, his presence filled the stage and she could tell from one look around that every woman in the place was just as mesmerized as she.

It was like something magical, something unreal, the power of his voice on the people was so strong. Then he looked at her, and what little reserves of strength she had fell away. She wasn't just close to falling for Riley. She was there. It was like she and he were the only people in that bar. All she could do was look into his eyes and listen to his voice and something so big swelled inside her, she felt she would burst from it.

It was the most profound moment of her life and the enormity of it brought tears to her eyes. When the last notes of the music died there was a couple of seconds of utter silence before the room erupted in cheers. Annie quickly swiped at her eyes and cheered along with everyone else.

"He's something isn't he?" Stella leaned over to say.

"He sure is."

"And a good friend. To Billy and all of us."

Annie heard the tone and recognized it. There was a warning here. She turned to face Stella. "He's seen his share of hard times, Annie. Made a world of mistakes and paid for every one of them. But he has made a good life for himself here. I think he's found peace, if not happiness. I'd hate to see anything harm that."

"I – I'd never do anything to hurt him. He's my friend."

The jukebox started up and people started filing onto the dance floor. Stella scooted over closer to Annie to kept from having to talk loud.

"I think he's a lot more than that, honey – even if you don't know it, it's right there on your face. So, if you don't mind, as a favor to me and the other people who love him – make sure your next step is taken for the right reasons. Hearts have a way of being broken and I'd hate to see that happen to either one of you."

Annie realized that Stella was not trying to warn her off Riley, but simply expressing her concern for a friend and she respected that. She knew Stella and all the Sweets were like family to Riley. "Thank you, Stella. I appreciate that. I don't want a broken heart either and I suspect if anyone has the power to do any breaking it's him."

Stella reached over and took her hand. "You've got a good heart, Annie. That's easy to see. I hope things work out."

Annie smiled and gave Stella's hand a squeeze. Just then Stella looked up, over Annie's shoulder and smiled. Annie turned her head to see Riley standing behind her. "Didn't you say something about dancing Wildcat girl?"

"Why yes I did, cowboy."

"Then may I?" He held out his hand.

"Indeed you may." She gave Stella's hand one final squeeze then stood and put her hand into Riley's. He whirled her onto the dance floor and for the next twenty minutes she was part of a country line dance party. Finally a slow song came on and Riley pulled her into his arms.

Annie looked up at him as he smoothly two-stepped her across the floor. He smiled down at her. "Having fun, Wildcat?"

She chuckled. "First you change my name to Annie and now it's Wildcat? There might not be a smidge of wild in me."

"Oh I'm betting there's a bit."

She shrugged, trying to pass it off rather than let him see what kind of thoughts that statement inspired. "Well, I guess that's for me to know."

"And me to find out?" He leaned down and whispered in her ear, pulling her closer.

She turned her head and could feel his breath on her face, feel his hand tighten on her hip. He moved just enough to look into her eyes. Annie took one look and was lost. Here it was, the fantasy man she'd dreamed of, asking a question that both thrilled and terrified her.

"Riley." It was all she could manage.

Riley had heard his name spoken in many ways – in the throes of passion, in the heat of anger, in the grips of fear and in the laughter of a friend, but he'd never heard those two syllables fall from someone's lips like a prayer, a wish buried so deep that the vocalization demanded a giving that went beyond words.

It annihilated him.

Everything around them faded. The music dulled, the sound of voices diminished and there was only them. In this moment. Both of his hands raised, as if of their own accord to cup her face. His lips met hers, soft and slow.

At the touch he felt her body weaken, leaning into him in what felt like surrender. Her lips were pliant and soft against his, hesitant at first, and then they parted ever so slightly. It was the invitation he sought and he answered it.

Her arms crept up, circling his neck, one hand working into his hair as the other gripped the collar of his shirt. Her full soft breasts pressed into his chest, the warmth seeping through.. She tasted of beer and barbecue, sweet and tangy all at once.

It was a kiss unlike any he'd ever experienced. There was passion and there was excitement, but there was… what was it? A reverence to it, a kind of giving he had no experience with. This kiss. This was what he'd searched for his whole life and never realized until this moment.

And it was in that moment that Riley fell. Annie Becke had him. Whether she wanted him or not, he was hers.

Annie nearly fell when the sudden sound of hoots, cheers and clapping pulled them apart. It was then that reality returned and she realized the entire bar of people was focused on the same thing. She and Riley.

131

She could feel heat flood her face and had no doubt that she was scarlet. And yet Riley had not released her. She dared to look up at him and saw him grinning at the people around him and then he looked down and grinned at her.

"You okay, Wildcat?"

"I – I'm not sure my legs work."

"Bit weak in the knees?"

"Just a bit."

"Same here, sugar."

"So what do we do?"

"We either have a beer and dance some more, or I take you home."

"To whose home?"

"You tell me."

She didn't know where she found the courage, but she found it and answered honestly. "Yours."

"Let me grab my guitar and we're outta here."

He turned to look around at the still cheering crowd. "Okay, show's over. Night ya'll."

With that he took her hand, led her toward the stage, grabbed his guitar and made for the door. They had just made it to the truck when he backed her up against the door for another kiss. Annie felt like a character out of a movie or a book. Could this really be her?

She returned the kiss with all the passion that had been bottled up inside her for so long. When he pulled back and looked at her, she knew he was excited. She'd felt that part of him pressing against her and it thrilled her.

"Ready to ride, Wildcat?"

"You have no idea."

Riley grinned, opened the door and she climbed in. He handed her his guitar, got in and started the truck. Annie cradled the guitar, watching as he drove. It should have felt strange that they rode without speaking, but the silence was not uncomfortable. Every now and then he'd look at her and smile, or reach over and caress her arm or leg.

It was wonderful and she both wanted the ride to be over and wanted it to stretch on. She knew that this moment would be one she'd remember forever. That wanting that filled the whole of her, and the anticipation of what was to come.

Whatever happened next, this moment would live in her memory forever as one of the most powerful of her life.

What she did not expect, was the impact that sent her careening into the window.

Chapter Ten

Rodrick stood when Giancarlo Moretti entered the room. He couldn't remember ever being this nervous, but then he'd never been invited to the home of the head of a crime syndicate. And who got invited for drinks at eleven o'clock at night?

"Mr. Becke, at last we meet." Giancarlo smiled as he crossed the room and extended his hand to Rodrick.

Rodrick clasped his hand, noticing how Giancarlo placed his left hand on top their clasped ones. It seemed a bit familiar for a first meeting. "It's an honor to meet you, Mr. Moretti."

"Please, call me Giancarlo. After all, if what my Gina tells me is true, we're going to be family."

Rodrick nearly swallowed his tongue. What the hell had Gina told her father? He forced a smile to his face and glanced at Gina, who was sitting on the sofa looking every bit like the cat that had swallowed the cream.

"I know we haven't made it formal and –" She lifted her left hand and waggled her fingers. "There's not a ring on my hand yet, but I just couldn't keep it to myself anymore, darling. Besides, you know it's important to me that you get Daddy's permission to make it official."

Rodrick wished for a hole to open up in the floor and swallow him. If his mind was still functional, Gina had just roped him into asking Giancarlo for her hand in marriage. He looked at Giancarlo and the look on the man's face told Rodrick he had not deduced incorrectly.

"I—forgive me. I had not quite anticipated this moment happening tonight and – and I fear I'm not quite prepared."

"What is there to prepare for?" Giancarlo asked and then gestured to the couch as he took a seat in a chair opposite the couch. "Please sit."

Rodrick sat stiffly beside Gina, wracking his brain for an appropriate response. He had to tread very carefully. Giancarlo Moretti was not just a savvy crime boss, he was a monster. Gina had boasted to Rodrick how her father's last wife had gotten *what she deserved*, when she tried to turn state's evidence against him.

Her body had been found nailed to a wall, literally, her eyes and tongue cut out and her body disfigured from burns that were ascertained to have been inflicted with a torch. In short she'd been tortured before shot in the head

Gina had taken pride in the fact that her father had carried out the torture personally. Her remark had been "the bitch got what she deserved." Rodrick was horrified. That sort of thing should be relegated to fiction. For someone to be that much of a psychopath was chilling. For his daughter to take such pride in it made her just as frightening and deadly.

. "Sir, "I – I wanted to be prepared with proof that I have the means to take care of Gina she deserves. My respect for her and for you demanded that I not formally ask you for your daughter"s hand in marriage until I proved proof that she would be taken care of in a manner she deserves and one that shows honor to you."

Giancarlo dismissed Rodrick's words with a wave of his hand. "I need no such proof, Ricky. I may call you Ricky? I am comfortable that there will be no indictments against you. And I do not need proof of a divorce. A

135

widower is a preferable state for a man who is to wed my only daughter."

Rodrick nearly threw up. He felt his gut clench and nausea rise up his throat. He swallowed hard, coughed and cleared his throat. "Pardon?"

"Daddy's simply stating the obvious, Ricky. If you have to drag it out in divorce court it will take forever, and when it comes to that Daddy always says that no one but the lawyers make out like bandits in divorce."

Giancarlo chuckled when Gina giggled at her own remark. Rodrick couldn't find any humor in any of it. They were talking about murdering his wife. "Sir, with all due respect, I believe I can make Analise see reason and –"

"I doubt that." Giancarlo interrupted. "You're talking with someone who has been through this more than once. Believe me, women are never satisfied regardless of what you offer. You either marry for life or come to peace with becoming a widower. Divorce is a hell no man can endure.

"Personally I prefer to gut them before they can cause me such annoyance, nevertheless, it is your decision. I understand that most of the funds your wife absconded with were put into your son's name. Somewhere in the neighborhood of twenty-three million?"

Rodrick cut Gina a look. It was like a kick to the head knowing that she'd told her father everything. He'd been insane about her for three years, dreamed about them having a life together. He thought she loved him, that she could be trusted. How wrong he'd been.

"Yes, about that." He didn't have the guts to do anything but answer.

"And surely you can speak with your son about returning the money."

"Uh, well, actually as I understand it, most of it was put into some kind of trust and Analise is the trustee."

"Interesting." Giancarlo got up and went to the bar to refresh his drink. "And I suppose that if something were to happen to your son – something like say, a tragic accident, the trust would revert to your wife?"

This time the fear had Rodrick bolting to his feet and looking around frantically for an exit. He spotted the door to the balcony and ran to it, flung it open and dashed across the to the railing, where he proceeded to vomit all over Manhattan.

When he had nothing left to retch, he spat, wiped his mouth and tried to compose himself. It was crystal clear that he was not just out of his depths, but swimming in shark infested waters. He couldn't sanction the murder of his family.

He whirled as he heard the click of heels behind him. Gina crossed the balcony to him. "Are you okay?"

"Fine. Fine. Just an upset stomach. Something I ate?"

"Are you sure?"

Her eyes glittered in the dim light and for the first time he saw her for who she was. Beneath that beauty and artifice was the soul of evil. Tonight wasn't meant to be a proclamation of their love and devotion. It was meant to be a test of his mettle.

She'd set him up by telling him about her father's last wife and the manner in which Giancarlo had disposed of her. It was a prelude to the demand that he act in a like manner. Get rid of Analise and David if that was what was her father demanded.

"I'm fine, darling." He turned away as he answered, afraid she'd see the lie on his face. He was anything but fine.

"Ricky, listen to me." She stepped up beside him and lowered her voice. "All you have to do is play along. My father can get make your problems vanish if you give him what he wants. So give it to him. Once you have his trust, we'll use your position and power to our advantage and gain a firmer hold in his empire."

He turned his head to look at her and she smiled. "You just have to prove your loyalty. I'm his only daughter, his little girl. He might be unwilling to hand over the reins of power to me, but not to you. You bring legitimacy to the table. And the ability to clean a lot of money. He's not stupid. He sees the advantage of having you in the family."

"And what advantage is that to us?" Was she campaigning for her father's benefit or her own?

"It positions us to take over."

"Take over?" Taking over a crime syndicate was the last thing in life he wanted.

"Yes. My brothers can be eliminated. Once they're gone I'm the sole heir. If you establish yourself as my father's right hand and something should happen to him then that enables me to take the throne. We'll have it all."

Rodrick pondered it briefly, forcing his mind into what it was most adept at, namely analytical thinking. At this point it did not come as a surprise that Gina wanted to use him to help her eliminate her father and wrest control of his empire. However, he didn't believe that her ambition would stop there. While she might end up as the heir to the kingdom, she would never be allowed to run the family syndicate. Other powerful families in the syndicate would see the Moretti family as weak if they were ruled by a woman.

She needed him as her puppet. She could never rule on her own and he'd never have the stomach for her way of life. She'd have to get rid of him and find a more suitable replacement. One she could control from behind the scenes but a man the rest of the syndicate would accept.

"We shouldn't discuss this here, Gina. Let's rejoin your father, shall we?"

"You're right. We don't want him to be suspicious, but you're with me, aren't you, Ricky?

"How could I not be?"

Her smile sent a chill sliding over his skin. He had to find a way to not just get away from her and her entire family, but a way to be safe from them. An idea occurred to him. It was risky and might land him in prison, but at this point prison seemed a step up from where he was headed with the Moretti family.

They returned inside. "I apologize. Must have been the shellfish at dinner. I don't feel one-hundred percent, so would you mind if we took this up at another time?"

"Of course, Ricky. Don't worry yourself about details. You're almost a part of the family and I always take care of family. Don't I, sweetheart?" He directed the last question to Gina.

"You better believe it. I'm going to go, too, Daddy. Why don't we all meet for dinner tomorrow. Your favorite restaurant? Nine, sound good?"

"Perfect. It's a date." He looked at Rodrick. "See you then...son."

Rodrick managed a nod. "Yes, sir. See you then."

The moment they were out of the penthouse, he looked at Gina. "Darling, I really am feeling unwell. Perhaps it would be best if you stayed at your place tonight – just in the off chance that this is something other than the shellfish. There is a nasty flu going around and I wouldn't want to infect you."

"Don't be silly, Ricky. Besides, I had my flu shot. And we have a lot to discuss." She pulled out her phone and summoned her driver. As they made their way to the elevator and during the ride down to the street level, Rodrick could think of only one thing – how to get away from Gina as quickly as possible and set his new plan into motion.

*****

Riley saw the blur of black headed toward them a split second before the impact, which gave him just enough time to stomp the accelerator. Lucky for him that was enough to have the oncoming car hit his truck just behind the driver's side door in the left rear panel, instead of on the door panel.

"Riley!" Annie screamed at the exact moment gunfire sounded.

The driver's side window exploded and he felt the spray of glass against the side of his face. A moment later the other window shattered.

"Hold on!"

The impact sent the back end of the truck skidding around to the right, threatening to go into a spin. Riley could have turned the steering wheel to halt the spin but instead, turned with it, braking just enough that the truck ended up behind the car that had hit him.

He punched the accelerator and Annie screamed again. "What are you doing? Are you crazy? We're going to—"

The rest of her words were cut short as the truck rammed the car from behind. It was enough to send the other car careening off the road and into the ditch.

Riley slammed on the brakes and threw his truck into park. He opened his door and felt Annie's hands on his arms. "What are you doing?"

"I'm going to find out why they ran into us. Just stay here."

"He's got a gun!"

"Just stay."

"No, I'm going with you."

"Annie, stay here." He pried her hands from his arm and climbed out of the truck. The driver of the car was just climbing out of the car when Riley reached it. There was no weapon in his hand.

"What the hell?" Riley yelled at him.

The man wasn't all that tall, but was stocky with a barrel chest and thick neck. "Fuck you, mother fuck—" That was all the man got out of his mouth before Riley punched him.

It stumbled the man back into the car door with blood spurting from his nose, but it didn't stop him. He pushed off the door and dove at Riley. It was like being hit by a bulldozer. Riley was lifted up off his feet and propelled backwards with the man bent over and plowing him like a football player determined to make a tackle.

Riley pounded on the man's back but it had no effect. His foot slipped and over backwards he went with the bulldozer on top of him.

A shriek preceded Annie suddenly pouncing on the bulldozer's back. She dug her fingernails into the man's face, gouging at his eyes.

Riley pressed the advantage her intervention provided and landed a few body blows. Luckily the man was soft in the middle, so it winded him. But not enough to stop him. He rolled off Riley, taking Annie with him.

She ended up under the man, screaming and kicking. Riley scrambled to his feet and kicked at the man's head. Bulldozer yowled and rolled off Annie. She wasted no time rolling over and scrambling away like a crab, getting to her feet as she moved.

Riley grabbed her and jerked her behind him. That's when Bulldozer hit again. Fists flew and they took it to the dirt with Annie getting in a few good kicks of her own. Twice the man made a lunge for Annie and twice Riley managed to drag her out of the way. The second time earned him a kidney punch that had him nearly going to his knees. The man had arms like a damn pile driver.

"Just give me the woman!" Bulldozer shouted as Riley came at him again.

There was no way in hell Riley would let that man get his hands on Annie. But his strength was waning. Bulldozer landed a punch to the side of Riley's head that had him spinning around and losing his balance. He went down and before he could recover the Bulldozer was on him.

Annie dove on the man's back but this time he flipped her over his head. Riley heard the expulsion of air from her as she hit the ground and then nothing. That scared him more than the three hundred pounds sitting on top of him and crushing him into the ground.

Big meaty hand wrapped around Riley's throat. A rapid succession of punches did nothing to loosen Bulldozer's hold. Between the man's weight on him and the choke hold, Riley's strength was fading fast.

"Stay down, motherfucker. You don't have to die. I just want the bitch."

Those words send a blast of fear induced adrenalin through him and Riley struggled harder. Bulldozer gave a roar and squeezed harder. That's when Riley's hand landed on something on the ground. A rock. Since he held to the notion that there was rarely such a thing as a fair fight, he used what was at his disposal, grabbed the rock and slammed in into his opponent's head.

God almighty, it took three hits to knock the bulldozer out. By the time Riley climbed to his feet, his legs were wobbly and he was splattered with blood. His and the bulldozer's.

Annie darn near took him down when she launched herself at him. He clutched her against him, feeling her heart pounding in competition to his. After a moment he gently pushed her back. "We have to call the law."

Her eyes widened. "Oh my god, you're bleeding. Riley, you're – oh my god, are you okay? You should sit down. We have to stop the bleed—"

"I'm okay. I'm fine. Please. We have to call the law." He felt for his phone. It wasn't there. Damn.

"You have your phone?

143

"It's in the truck."

"Get it and call 911."

She ran to the truck and returned in seconds with the phone. He didn't question when she handed it to him. Riley quickly dialed 911 as he turned to eye the unconscious man on the ground twenty feet from the truck. "Hey, this is Riley Morgan. I'm on Old Cotton Gin road, about a mile from the Creekside bridge. We were hit and I have an unconscious man on the ground. I need an ambulance and the Sheriff. This wasn't an accident. We were deliberately hit."

He didn't wait for instructions. He just ended the call, handed her the phone and made for the truck. Riley grabbed his shotgun from behind the seat, racked in two loads and stood leaning against the crumpled back panel of the truck where he could see the man and look down the road every few seconds.

Annie leaned on the truck beside him and he wrapped one arm around her. He could feel her trembling. "Are you okay?"

"I think." She rubbed at her head and he heard a sharp intake of breath. When he looked down he saw the blood on her hand. Riley quickly turned to take a look. Sure enough, she had a nice gash in her head on the right side. That was probably going to need stitches.

"We've got to get you looked at."

"No. I'm okay. But you need a doctor, Riley. You're bleeding worse than I am. There's at least two deep cuts on the left side of your face and your mouth and nose are all bloody. You need medical attention."

"I'll be fine. The police will be here soon. Just hold on."

"Okay."

It felt like an eternity before he heard the sound of sirens in the still night. A blink of an eye later, Annie's body went limp. He manage to drop the shotgun and catch her before she fell.

Just as he was sweeping her up into his arms a police car skidded to a stop, billowing dust. Deputy Greene jumped out just as the firetruck and ambulance pulled up behind him. "You okay, Riley? Ms. Becke?"

"She needs to be looked at. Took a good lick to the head."

Riley carried her to the ambulance. "Check her out."

"Sure, Riley." One of the EMT's stepped aside for Riley to carry Analise into the ambulance and place her on the gurney. Her eyes opened and she latched onto his hand.

"You're okay. You're okay. You're in an ambulance. They're going to take you to the hospital to check you out and when I'm done here I'll come and find you."

"No. I'm not leaving. Not without you."

Riley held up his hand to the EMT and knelt down beside Analise. "Look, I need to tell them what happened and you need to get checked out. As soon as I talk to the Deputy I'll meet you at the hospital."

"No, you shouldn't be driving. You're all – you're bleeding. You need to be checked out. Sir? Sir! You need to check him. He's—"

"Annie listen to me." Riley had to shout to get her to listen. When she fell silent he lowered his voice. "Listen. I'm okay. I just need to talk to the Deputy and I promise I'll come to the hospital."

145

"No. If you're staying, I'm staying."

"Annie."

"I said I'm staying." She crossed her arms over her chest and that was an action Riley understood all too well. Nothing said intractable and unmoving like a woman with her arms crossed over her chest.

"Fine, then will you please at least let Dave there check you out and wait on me in the ambulance?"

For a moment he thought she was going to refuse but finally she nodded. "Okay."

Riley gave her a kiss on the cheek and nodded to the EMT." How 'bout checking her out and waiting for me?"

"You got it."

Riley climbed out of the ambulance and made his way back to the Deputy who had the unconscious man rolled over on the ground and handcuffed. "I think we're going to need another ambulance. I don't want to send him with Ms. Becke."

"I'll drive her over to the hospital when we're done here."

"Then let me get him loaded up."

It took a few minutes to get the man loaded into the ambulance. Annie refused to get in the truck. She sat on the tailgate with her eyes on Riley. It was another twenty minutes before Riley finished telling the Deputy what happened.

"You're sure he said he wanted her?" the Deputy asked.

"Yeah. Twice."

"Why?"

Riley cut a look at Annie before answering. "Her husband is apparently in trouble with some mob guys in New York."

"Mob?"

"Yeah. Apparently Mr. Becke stole from them."

The Deputy nodded. "I think that's all for now. I need to search the car."

"Want some help?"

"You can join but I'd prefer you don't touch anything."

"Whatever you say."

They approached the car and the Deputy Greene leaned down to look inside the open car door. "There's a gun on the floorboard."

"I told you he shot at us."

"Don't touch anything." Deputy Greene hurried to his car. When he returned he was wearing latex gloves and carrying evidence bags. He retrieved the gun, bagged it and laid it on the roof of the car. Next he bagged two cell phones.

Taking the keys from the ignition, he opened the trunk. Inside was a laptop and a Kindle. He bagged those and took all of the evidence to his squad car.

"What're you going to do with all that?" Riley asked.

"See if there's anything that will help us determine what this is all about. The phone was locked so we may have to call in help from the county."

"I know someone who can unlock it."

147

"Oh?" Deputy Greene's eyebrows rose.

"He's not a criminal. Just really good with this kind of thing. He works for me. Bobby."

"I need to check with the Chief on this. Text me his phone number and if we can't get someone from the County, I'll see if the Chief will approve me calling him in."

"Okay. Anything else you need from me, Tom?"

"Yeah, I need you to get Ms Becke to the hospital. And get yourself checked out, Riley. You look like you've been run over by a truck."

"Or a bulldozer. I will. Thanks, Tom."

Riley returned to Annie. She was slumped against the bed of the truck. "Come on, honey. Let's get you to the hospital."

"Thanks." She wobbled as she stood and he put an arm around her for support. Riley helped Annie into his truck and started out behind the ambulance carrying the unconscious attacker.

After a couple of miles during which she hadn't spoken he looked over at her. "Annie, you okay?"

She didn't answer. Riley reached over and shook her and she still didn't answer. A bit of panic had him wanting to pass the ambulance and haul ass as fast as he could to the hospital, but good sense told him that the last thing they needed tonight was another mishap.

Chapter Eleven

Riley sat up, rolled his shoulders, then took off his hat and propped his elbows on his knees. He let his hands fall between his legs, holding onto his hat. He'd been sitting in the chair by Annie's bed for two days.

As it turned out, she did have a concussion. They'd kept her awake until they felt it was safe for her to sleep. She had been grazed by the bullet that shattered the window, had cuts from the glass, some bruised ribs and a dislocated shoulder. The bullet wound had been treated, as had the cuts, but they waited until they felt it safe to sedate her before setting her dislocated shoulder. She'd been out for nearly thirteen hours.

Riley had done a lot of thinking during the long hours of waiting. Annie had gotten to him in a big way. It'd been a long time since he'd let himself care about someone and hadn't intended to care for her, but she'd blown down his defenses without effort. Last night he'd fully intended to take her to his home, to make love to her.

Today he didn't know what to do. On one side of the coin was the way she'd acted when they were hit. She dove into the fight without a care for herself. It almost brought a smile to his face, thinking how she'd lit into the big man. And afterwards her concern had been for him rather than herself.

The other side of the coin wasn't much to smile about. The police had uncovered some interesting information about the man who ran into them. Information that led him to believe that being around Analise Becke was dangerous.

He needed to tell Cody, tell all the Sweets. They deserved to know everything so they could decide if they wanted Annie to continue staying at the ranch. Hell, he needed to tell Annie. He needed to look into her eyes when he told her and see if the news surprised her. He hoped to god it did, because if it didn't then that meant she had willingly put him and the entire Sweet family in harm's way.

Analise woke and blinked in confusion. Where was she? It took a few seconds to remember what had happened. Her eyes moved around the room and she saw Riley sitting in a chair beside the bed, slumped over with his elbows on his knees. She watched him for a few minutes.

When she'd seen him fight that man, she'd experienced something primal. Despite her fear, she wasn't willing to risk injury to rush to his aid.

Later, seeing the blood on his face and splattered on his clothes had scared her half to death. She hadn't given a thought to whether she was intact or injured. All she could think about was him. She'd been sitting on the tailgate of his truck, waiting on him when it hit her. She didn't just have a crush on a movie star. She'd fallen in love with Riley. He'd been her friend for over a year, a friend whom she respected and admired. He was a man she admired. Regardless of what his life had been when he was Nate Bridges, as Riley Morgan he was the kindest and most honorable man she'd ever known. He made her want to be just as good as him.

Not to mention that he lit a fire inside her like nothing she'd ever experienced. She'd met Rodrick when she was an inexperienced girl. He was handsome and wealthy and it was exciting to be pursued. He was her first lover and she'd never had another.

But she'd never felt the kind of desire for Rodrick that Riley inspired. She dreamed of Riley, of his touch and wanted him more than she knew how to handle.

Now, looking at him, sitting there slumped over, she wanted only to comfort him, to ease any worry or strain, to take care of him. She reached out and ran her fingers over his hair.

Riley felt her touch and looked up. Her fingers drifted away but not before trailing over the side of his face. The concern he saw on her face filled him with dread and a fair measure of guilt.

"Are you okay?"

"Yeah, I'm fine, honey."

"Are you sure? Riley, don't lie to me. That man... I thought he was going to kill you. When I saw him on top of you—"

"I'm okay, Annie."

"How long have we been here,?"

"Two days."

"Two days? That's not possible. I was just--"

"You had a concussion. And you were grazed by the bullet that shattered the windows and have bruised ribs, some cuts from the glass and your shoulder was dislocated. Do you remember any of it?"

"I remember something. People telling me I couldn't sleep and doing things to my head. A machine? They were running tests or something. It's kind of foggy. I was so tired."

"Yeah, they had to keep you awake for a while until the swelling went down and it was safe for you to sleep."

"How long have I been asleep?"

"About thirteen hours."

"It's morning?'

"Yep. Half past nine."

"Are you sure you're okay?"

"I'm fine.

"Riley."

There it was. Again. Two little syllables he'd heard more times than he could count in his life, yet when spoken by her had the power to incite something inside him that he didn't know how to control. He straightened in his chair, steeling himself.

"Annie. We have to talk."

"About what happened?"

"No, about the man who ran into us."

"Okay." She fumbled for the remote to raise the bed into a sitting position.

"Deputy Greene ran the man's license and finger prints through the database and the guy's a criminal."

"A criminal?"

"Yeah, been in and out of prison several times and is apparently associated with some big time criminals in New York."

Her eyebrows drew together in a frown. "What would someone like that be doing here?"

"Apparently trying to grab you."

"Me?" She shook her head. "That's crazy. I don't know any criminals."

"No, but I think your husband does."

His words sent a jolt through her that had her sitting up straight as a rod, wincing at the pain in her shoulder and down her side. "What?"

"Apparently the guy who rammed us, Leo Scarletti, has been known to work for Giancarlo Moretti. And Moretti owns companies that do business with your husband's company, Becke Ltd. Which is, by the way, under investigation by the Federal Trade Commission and the Department of Justice."

He reached over to take her hand. "Annie, the police recovered a cell phone from the car and thanks to a friend were able to unlock it. There are calls between the guy who attacked us and this Moretti guy. Also, they recovered a laptop and a Kindle belonging to you. Do you have any idea how the guy got those things? I called Cody and she said your laptop is still in your room at her ranch.

She looked down, twisting the wedding ring on her finger around and around. She knew that what she said next would affect everything between her and Riley. She felt pulled in two directions. On the one hand, she didn't want to sell Rick short. She still held out hope that whatever his family was involved in, he was an unwitting accomplice. To think that the man she's spent half her life with was a criminal was a bitter pill to swallow.

However, on the other hand, she and Rick had not had a true marriage in years. He'd been cheating on her for a good while and she had stopped caring about the lack of affection or attention. If he was innocent of wrong doing the investigation would uncover that. If he was guilty, well in this case, she had no sympathy for him because it would mean he'd chosen to do something illegal.

In the end what mattered to her now was her son, and Riley. She was in love with him and he was an honorable man. He deserved the truth. She looked back up to find him watching her.

"When I was at the writer's convention someone broke into my room. They sliced up all my clothes and took my laptop and Kindle. I and the police chalked it up to a random act."

"You never mentioned it."

"I know. I'm sorry. I thought it was just – well, random."

"And your husband?"

"I know about the family business being under investigation. I told you, remember? I mean at the time there was the threat of an investigation. I didn't know it had actually happened."

"It has."

"I'm sorry, but what does that have to do with us getting rammed?"

"Apparently it's connected. That man who attacked us. He had your things and he wanted you. He said so. Are you sure you don't know why?"

"I don't. God is my witness, I don't Riley. If it was the man who broke into my room in San Antonio, I can't even imagine why. And I was never privy to any of Rick's business dealings. Hell, for the last ten years I don't think he even remembered I existed until he needed to throw a party or entertain a client and then he just assumed I would handle it."

"Did you ever meet Moretti?"

"No. I never heard the name until you said it."

"So, you don't think Moretti being involved with your husband and the investigation could have anything to do with a gangster showing up in Cotton Creek and trying to kill us?"

"No. I mean what's the point? I'm not part of Rick's business. I don't know a thing about it. And ...and I told you that he's been having an affair for the last few years with some young woman so it's not like someone could use hurting me as leverage against him."

"You sure about that?"

"Well, I don't think he would want to see me hurt but I – oh my god." The lights suddenly clicked on in her muddled brain as the pieces came together. "David!"

"Your son?"

"Yes. Where's my phone? I need my phone."

Riley got up and looked in the tiny cupboard. There was a plastic bag inside containing Annie's belongings. He handed the phone to her. "Someone tried to call you."

"It was Rick." She quickly accessed the voice mail, turned on the speakerphone and hit play.

Rick's voice came through the speaker. "Analise, it's Rick. Wherever you are, you have to call me. You have to give that money back. Now. It's vital, Analise. Life and

155

death. Call me. And call David. I can't reach him. Just make sure – make sure he's okay. Call me Analise. Call me."

Analise looked at Riley. "I have to call David."

She quickly placed the call. David answered on the third ring. "Hey Mom, what's up?"

"David, are you okay?"

"Yeah. Why?"

"Have you heard from your father?"

"He's called a couple of times but I've been busy so I haven't talked with him."

"Where are you now?"

"Headed home from class."

"Okay, well do me a favor and call me when you get there, okay?"

"Sure, or we can talk on the ride."

"No, I've – I've got a bad connection anyway. Just-- just be careful and call me back."

"Okay, will do."

"Okay, I love you."

"Love you too, Mom."

She ended the call and looked at Riley. "I'm scared. Should I have kept him on the phone? What if--?"

"Don't panic. Chances are he'll be fine and he'll call back shortly. But what was that bit about the money that your husband was talking about?"

The last thing she wanted was to discuss the details of her marriage with Riley, but she didn't see any way to avoid it. "Before I left, I took half of what Rick had in several offshore accounts and put it into a trust for our son, David. And I cleaned out two joint savings accounts we had and put it in my own account."

"How much money are we talking about, Annie?"

"For me, it was close to a million."

"And the rest?"

"Twenty-three million."

Riley blew out his breath and took a seat. "Twenty three million dollars?"

She nodded. A picture was starting to form in her head and it wasn't a pretty one. In fact, it was one that was starting to terrify her. "Riley, I have to get out of here. I have to get my son somewhere safe and I have to do it now."

She started to get out of the bed, but he stopped her. "Hold on. Just hold on. Before you do anything, I want you to explain things to me. You said you took half of what your husband had in those offshore accounts, which means there was sixty-four millions dollars stashed away."

"Yes."

"Was that honest money?"

There was the question she didn't know the answer to and didn't really want to know. "I don't know. Especially now. With what happened to us – what the police told you and now that message from Rick. I think he may have gotten himself into some deep trouble with some bad people.

"And color me having a big imagination, but I'm scared that's what has happened. And if those people want their money, they'll come after me and David."

"Because you have the money? "

"No. Because David has it. And if he dies, the trust reverts to me. Unless…"

"Unless you're dead."

Analise nodded. "I have to get my son to safety."

"Yes. You do."

"So, you'll get me out of here?"

"I will, but before I do you have to answer one more question."

"Okay."

"Where will you go? And if you run, won't it make it look like you're part of whatever your husband is into?"

"Excuse me?"

"To the feds. Surely you have to know that they're watching you as well. You are married to the man."

"And in the process of divorcing him."

"But still married."

"Shit. Shit, shit, shit." If she booked David an airline ticket, her credit card could be traced and it would be easy to figure out where he was. "Oh my god, Riley, what do I do? He's my child. I have to protect him."

"I think you need to call the FBI and tell them everything you know."

"Are you serious?"

"Dead serious."

She thought about it, but only for a few seconds. He was right. She was innocent so there was nothing to fear. She hadn't known where the money came from that she took from Rick and she would turn it over to the law if that's what it took.

"You're right. I just want to make sure David is safe. He hasn't done anything and if something were to happen—" She couldn't even finish the sentence. The enormity of it all hit her like a freight train.

The tears came, in torrents, accompanied by sobs she tried to muffle by covering her face with her hands. She'd never known fear like this. Her entire being was consumed by it.

Whatever doubts Riley had harbored were gone. He wasn't a mind reader, but he was pretty good at reading people and he knew she was being truthful with him. What he saw now was an innocent woman who'd gotten caught up in something out of her control and a mother who was in fear for her child's life.

However foolish it was, that brought out something in him that didn't emerge too often. The need to be a hero. He knew in that instant that he was going to do whatever it took to save both Annie and her son.

"Annie, honey." He moved to sit on the bed and gather her into his arms. "I'm here. I'm here and we'll get through this. We'll make sure David is safe. I promise."

"How can you promise that?" Her words were choked with tears.

"Because I believe in you." He pushed her back and held her at arm's length. "Now listen to me. I can get David here. I'm not without friends and I can get him here safely. You and he will move to the ranch with me where I can keep an eye on you.

"We'll call the FBI and get them to send whoever they need to send to talk to you and you can tell them everything you know. And whatever happens, I'll be right here with you. All the way."

Analise had never loved anyone more than she loved Riley in that moment. What he was offering was so huge it was almost unbelievable and she realized it was a true gift of love. But she also knew that she couldn't let him put himself in harm's way. It wasn't a matter of worrying that something might happen and she'd never be able to forgive herself, it was a matter of allowing him to put himself in whatever cross-hairs there were out there for her and David.

She wiggled out of his grasp and straightened as best she could. "Riley, I – god, I don't even know how to start to tell you what that means to me, but I can't."

"You can't what?"

"I can't let you put yourself in danger for me. I need to leave and I mean leave Cotton Creek. I'm not going to bring trouble down on you or anyone else here. It's not right."

"It is right and you're not letting me do anything. I'm offering."

"Why?" She suddenly needed to hear him say it. "Why would you do that?"

"Because you're my –"

"Friend? Riley, this goes way beyond the call of friendship."

"You're right."

"Then why?"

He looked at her and once more she was caught in that timeless moment, lost in his eyes and filled with emotion so overwhelming that it nearly robbed her of her breath. His right hand moved up to cup the side of her face.

"You know why, Annie."

"I need to hear it."

His eyes searched hers and he moved closer, never breaking eye contact. "Because I'm falling in love with you."

The whole world went silent and shrunk to the size of that one small room. Nothing else existed, there were no other thoughts in her head except for the echo of his words. Then another thought crept in. Was this real? Maybe she'd died in that crash. Maybe she was in a coma dreaming this.

"Could you pinch me please?"

"Pardon?"

"Pinch me, Riley."

"Why? Is something wrong? Do you feel –"

"I just need to know this is real."

He sagged visibly. "Damn Annie, you scared me."

"I'm sorry but – but you said…"

"I said I'm falling in love with you."

"As in you like me and that like could be more in time, or you've already moved into the something more but it's not quite certain, or you think you might –"

"I love you."

Her mouth stopped working. He loved her? Riley Morgan loved her?

"Annie?"

"I – oh god, Riley, it doesn't feel real."

"Why?"

"Why? Because … because you're you. You're the guy on the movie screen, the one I dreamed about for so long, the one I cooked up fantasies about. You're him and you're you – you're the two men I base everything that's perfect about a man on, the one I write about and dream about and want more than anything."

"Well, here I am honey. Telling you that I love you and waiting to hear that I'm not in this by myself."

There was no thought for her injuries. Analise launched herself off the bed and onto his lap, her arms curling around his neck. "I love you, Riley Morgan."

He smiled just before he kissed her, and it was *the* kiss of her dreams. The kiss that promised passion, comfort, companionship, friendship, protection and love. It promised all of that, but more than anything it promised what she wanted most of all. Home.

Not home as in a place to hang her hat, but home as in that one person you can invest everything in, that person you can bare your soul before and know that whatever your shortcomings, you will be forgiven and whatever your strengths you will be respected.

Riley's kiss, his arms tight around her – it said *here is your home* – and she latched onto it knowing that she would never willingly let go.

For that one brief moment, life was more wonderful than anything she'd ever dreamed. And then reality returned.

She pulled back from him. "I love you, Riley, and that's why I have to leave here."

"No. You're not leaving. Now listen to me. I have a friend who works for the Justice Department. I'm going to call him and get him to fly to wherever your son is and bring him here and then you're going to tell him everything you know. About your husband, his business and that money you took."

"You don't think I'll go to jail do you?"

"No. I don't. But I do think you have to tell them everything you know."

"I know and I will, but if that crime boss or whatever he is sent that guy down here, who's to say he won't send someone else? Riley, I can't let you or anyone here be put in harm's way."

"You're not asking. I'm telling. You're staying with me. You and David. And I'll protect you."

"But what if someone tried to do something to Cody or her family?"

"We're going to let the police chief know what's going on. And the Sweets. Hell I'm gonna let everyone I know hear the truth."

"I don't know that I want everyone knowing."

Riley fell silent for a minute, his eyes searching hers. "You come from a small town, right?"

"Yes."

"And in that small town, what would the people do if someone threatened one of their own?."

"Today? I don't know. I've been gone a long time."

"So when you were a kid."

"Well, I guess they'd stand together. At least most of them."

"And that's what we do here. Trust me on this, Annie. Cotton Creek folks look out for their own."

"I'm not one of their own, Riley."

"But I am. And you're mine."

"Am I?"

"Do you want to be?"

"I do."

"Then it's settled. Now, get back in that bed while I go find your doctor and see about getting you out of here."

She gave him a kiss on the cheek, did as he requested and got back into the bed. Her mind went into a whirl. If Rodrick and his family had taken money from someone in organized crime and that person was trying to use her and David as a threat to get their money back, maybe the safest bet was just to give them what they wanted.

Then again, if she did that, did it make her an accomplice to something illegal? She wished she knew the answers. She wished David was here with her where she could see that he was safe. And she wished Riley would hurry up and get back.

Chapter Twelve

Rodrick felt like the only guppy at a shark convention. Gina, her father Giancarlo, and two of Giancarlo's associates sat around the table in the conference room of one of Giancarlo's businesses. Rodrick could feel sweat trickle down the center of his chest, his back and sides.

Giancarlo had just laid the cards on the table. He wanted the rest of his money and he wanted it now. He'd sent a man to Texas to take care of Analise but the man failed. So now it was up to Rodrick to take care of things. Get the money. By any means necessary. I

"Bring me the bitch's head," were his final words.

It took every ounce of self control he could muster to keep from leaping from his chair and fleeing. Rodrick was terrified as he looked around the table at the people assembled. "I understand. I'll make arrangements to leave as soon as possible."

"No need." Giancarlo nodded to one of his associates who slid an envelope across the table to Rodrick. Inside was an airline ticket.

"Tony will be accompanying you, Ricky. For protection."

Rodrick looked at the man who'd given him the ticket. Tony. He knew from talking with Gina that Tony's job was enforcing Giancarlo's will. Which meant that if Rodrick didn't get the job done, Tony would. Only Tony would add Rodrick to the body count.

"Understood. Will there be anything else?"

"No, that's all Ricky. Have a safe flight."

"Thank you sir."

As he stood, so did Gina. She followed him outside. "Ricky, you have to get this done. For us."

"I know. I will." He didn't believe the words coming out of his mouth but hoped she did. He couldn't even think about doing what was demanded of him.

"Promise?"

"When have I ever let you down?" It was the safest response he could muster at the moment. His heart was beating way too fast and nausea was bubbling up his throat. He was scared he was going to have a heart attack.

She kissed him and for a split second the passion she inspired almost washed away the misery, fear and guilt. Almost. Then he remembered who she was.

"Hurry back to me, Ricky."

He nodded and turned away. If he was lucky, very lucky, he'd never see Gina or her father again.

*****

Analise was nervous, for several reasons. First there was the fact that Rodrick had apparently gotten himself into serious trouble, not only with the government but with people in organized crime. Second, she was on her way to Riley's where she would be staying.

She looked over at Cody who was behind the wheel of her old red pick-up. Cody had argued that Analise could continue to stay with her. She could protect Analise just as well as Riley. He was having no part of that. Analise would be staying with him. As would her son, David, as soon as he arrived. Cody had managed to convince him to let her pick Annie up from the hospital and bring her to his ranch.

So now, here Analise was, her belongings jostling around in the back of Cody's truck, about to get her first look at Riley's home. "So, you haven't really said much about what I told you, Cody."

"What's to say? Your ex is an idiot who got himself into a mess and it's threatening to spill over onto you. But Riley's friend in the Justice Department is going to bring your kid here and you'll both be safe at Riley's."

"You make it sound so simple."

"Sometimes it is. You just gotta believe, Annie. Look, you haven't done anything wrong so the Feds don't have any bone to pick with you. You can turn over the money you took from your ex to them and you'll be out of the picture."

"It's not the government that concerns me."

"You mean the goons?" Cody scoffed. "Girl, please, you're in Texas and we protect what's ours. If anyone shows up here threatening you, they're gonna be in for a world of hurt."

"I don't want anyone getting hurt."

"No one's going to be. Trust me, Annie. It's all going to be okay. You just have to have a little faith."

Analise nodded and turned to look out of the passenger side window. She wanted to believe that everything would be all right, that there would be no danger to David or to anyone here in Cotton Creek, but she was still scared.

"Here we are." Cody announced as she braked to make a right turn onto a dirt road.

Analise perked up, paying more attention as they made their way up the road. Pasture fence lined both sides

167

of the road. A few scraggly dotted the pastures and she saw quite a few cows in the pasture on the left side of the road.

As the house came into view she leaned forward a bit. She's tried so many times to imagine it in her mind and it wasn't what she'd anticipated. She reminded herself that her mental images of Riley and his ranch had been formed before she realized he was also Nate Bridges. She'd thought him to be a small rancher who probably had little excess and lived in an old home.

The house was big and in pristine shape. It reminded her of an old country farm house, with a wide, wraparound porch. Dormer windows graced the second story of the front of the house. Painted a soft sand color with darker trim, the home gave the appearance of stability and comfort.

It could have been built last week or a hundred years ago. As they got closer she realized just how big it was. On the other side of the drive stood several structures, two large barns and three other smaller buildings.

There were horses in the pasture near the house, several pick-up trucks and a tractor parked near one of the larger barns. Riley's truck was parked near the house.

Cody pulled up behind his truck and stopped. "I'll help you get your stuff moved inside."

"Thanks, Cody." Analise reached for the door handle and just as she did, Riley stepped out of the house onto the front porch.

It literally took her breath. How she wished this was the sight she would always see, him coming out of the house to meet her as she came home. She scolded herself for her romantic yearnings and got out of the truck.

She waved and walked to meet him. Nothing could have surprised her more than for him to scoop her up in a hug. "Welcome home, Annie."

Once more she had that yearning inspired vision of happily-ever-after and for a moment she indulged herself, returning the hug. "Thank you so much for letting me stay here."

"I wouldn't have it any other way." He set her back on her feet and released her. " Now, let's get you settled in. Looks like Cody's trying to pack mule everything in one trip."

Analise laughed as she looked Cody's way. Sure enough, Cody was laden. She had a box under her right arm, and was pulling a piece of luggage with the same hand. There was a box in her other arm, with a stack of clothes on hangers tossed on top.

"You leave us anything to carry, half-pint?" Riley asked as he walked by her to look into the bed of the truck.

"Few things. Where do you want these?"

"Just take them inside and put them in the den. We'll get them squared away."

"You got it."

Analise grabbed the messenger bag containing her laptop and tablet, her purse and a small travel case from the back, leaving Riley to get the last two boxes.

"I spoke with David just before we left the hospital. Your friend, Kade and a woman, Cia, I think was her name, flew up and met him last night. They're leaving today. David said that Kade and Cia think it's best if they drive. They don't want to take a chance on alerting anyone of David's movements."

Riley nodded. "Yeah, Kade called a few minutes ago. Said it would take about 4 days. They're not gonna push it and want to make sure David's not being followed."

"Do they think he might be?"

"They aren't sure. The department they work with doesn't normally handle this kind of case, but the head of the division said he'd make an exception, so they have a team of people looking into your husband and his associates, along with that mob guy."

Analise blew out a breath. "As much as it scared me to think about going to the police, I'm glad you called your friend. I guess he'll want to talk to me when he gets here?"

"Said he would. You okay with that?"

"Yes."

He stopped at the first step of the porch to face her. "You sure?"

Analise nodded. "I am."

"Well, all righty then. Let's get this stuff in and get you settled."

She smiled and followed him inside. Yesterday she hadn't been sure she was okay with talking to the FBI about Rick, but she'd lain awake all night thinking about it. Even if it meant giving back the money she'd taken and put in trust for David, she knew it was the right thing to do.

If Rick and his family had stolen from people, the money needed to be returned. If they'd stolen from some mob guy then the money was tainted and she didn't want it anyway. She had enough to help David, and her book sales were earning her a decent living so they'd both be okay.

The moment she stepped inside Riley's house she stopped cold. "Oh my."

It was beautiful. Warm and inviting. The front room stretched the entire width of the house. Warm terracotta tile for flooring was scattered with thick rugs. An enormous fireplace dominated the right side wall and was balanced with deep cushioned furniture in earth tones. The seating area took up the entire right side of the large room, while a beautifully polished and quite large dining set occupied the left side of the room.

"This is beautiful, Riley."

"Thanks." He gestured to the framed opening on the rear wall of the room. "Kitchen's though there to the right and my room to the left. Upstairs has three bedrooms, all with their own baths. Laundry is behind the kitchen."

"Can I look?"

"Sure, but don't you want to put your stuff away?" He looked over at Cody who was piling stuff on the couch. "Might as well bring that to the bedroom."

"Which one?"

Analise noticed the way he hesitated before he responded. "The front room upstairs." He started for the framed opening. A short hall held another opening to the kitchen. Across from it was a door that she could see into as they passed. Riley's room. A staircase was at the end of the hall.

He led the way up the stairs. It was not so much a hall as a niche, with doors on all three walls. Riley went through the center door and she followed. It was an enormous room, with two dormer windows, probably the ones she saw when she arrived. A big poster bed sat between the windows with nightstands flanking each side.

171

There was a large dresser on the wall adjacent to the door and a dressing vanity graced the adjoining wall.

On the other side of the door was a sitting area and a door leading into a well-appointed bathroom. Riley put her things on the bed and got out of the way as Cody dumped the load she carried onto the bed.

"Okay, I gotta bolt."

"Thank you for bringing me." Analise put down her things on the bed and went to Cody to give her a hug. "And for putting me up."

"Don't mention it. House's never been so clean and I'm damn sure gonna miss your cooking."

"Well, maybe I'll get lucky and she'll do some cooking here." Riley interjected. "And if she does you're welcome anytime, half-pint."

"Thanks, bud. Okay, I'm outta here. Call me later Annie?"

"You know I will."

She and Riley watched Cody leave and then an awkward silence fell. She wasn't sure what to say and apparently neither was he. Words had been spoken between them and she feared it was those words that were making them both uncomfortable.

"Look, I know you probably have stuff to do, so don't let me hold you up. Is it okay to put my stuff in the closet?"

"Put it wherever you want. This is your home – I mean until – you know."

"I do. Thank you. And maybe after that, I could take a walk around your ranch?"

"Absolutely. Okay, I'll leave you to it." He gave her a kiss on the cheek and turned to leave.

Just as he reached the door she called out to him. "Would it be okay if I fixed dinner?"

"Girl, I never turn down a home-cooked meal. Just go through the kitchen and fix whatever you want."

"Okay, thanks. What time do you want to eat?"

"I like to eat early – around seven? I should be done by six and that'll give me time to clean up and have a beer."

"Perfect."

"And I have my phone if you need me."

"I'll be fine. Thanks."

"Okay, see you later."

"Yep."

She watched him leave before going to one of the windows and looking out. It wasn't long before she saw him walk out into the front yard. He stopped and looked back, his gaze going to the window where she stood.

Analise's breath caught in her throat as their gazes locked. Finally she collected her wits enough to raise one hand and wave. He returned the wave with a smile before continuing on his way. She watched until he disappeared around the side of the barn and then sat down on the bed.

Staying here was going to be a challenge. She knew she was in love with him, but she was afraid to make too much out of it, despite his confession to her. What she wanted to do was to jump him. What she should do was to take it slow, let their friendship come back to the foreground. That's where they were comfortable and at ease with one another.

The problem was, her damn libido was not just a single drum solo. She had a whole freaking drumline hammering at her. How crazy was that? Her and her son's life were in danger from the mob and she was lusting after Riley.

*****

Riley sat down on the back porch and pulled off his boots. Telling his guys about the possible threat had not been at the top of his list of happy moments for the day. God bless 'em, every one, to a man, vowed support and vigilance and he walked away feeling like a damn lucky guy.

At least in some respects. He stood with his boots in his hands and turned toward the back door. There was a woman in his house, one he'd known for a year as a friend, and one he'd fallen in love with faster than was wise.

A woman who was in danger and one he wanted to protect. Was it the need to protect that had him feeling so strongly about her? He didn't think so. She pretty much had him the first time he saw her standing there in the road beside that broken down RV.

He knew he liked her, knew that he wanted her and was almost certain he was falling in love with her. And that was the rub. He'd fallen in love before. Three of those times he'd married the woman, and all three times it had ended badly. Riley thought of it in baseball terms. Three strikes and you're out. Maybe love wasn't meant for him. At least not the lasting kind.

Which left him with a decision. The first option was to backtrack and tell her he wasn't in love with her, but cared for her as friend and hope he could save the friendship. The second choice was to go with what he was feeling and hope they didn't end up like all of his other relationships.

Seemed that both options carried a strong chance of him losing – either her friendship or her entirely. Damn, he wished he knew what to do. He opened the backdoor, put his boots down beside it and padded in his sock feet to the kitchen, intending on grabbing a beer and getting a shower.

What met his eyes had him forgetting all about that beer. Annie was standing at the butcher block in the center of the kitchen, with her back to him, preparing a salad. She had music playing and was singing along as she worked.

There was an amazing aroma coming from the kitchen and he could see through to the dining room where two places had been set. There were even candles on the table. Riley leaned against the doorway and just watched.

This was something he'd fantasized about more than once, what it would be like to have someone to come home to. Only it was better. Those choices he'd been pondering two minutes ago vanished like mist in the morning sun. This was what he wanted. This place, this woman and this kind of moment to come home to every night.

Analise gathered up the cutting board, knife and scraps from the vegetables and went to the sink, still singing. Once she'd disposed of the cuttings and washed the cutting board and utensils she picked up a dish towel to dry her hands and turned.

"Riley." Her smile lit something warm inside him. "I didn't hear you come in."

"Something smells amazing."

Her smile hitched up a notch in brightness. "I hope you'll like it. Oh, you want a beer?"

"I think I'll get cleaned up first."

"Okay. I'll just pop the salad into the refrigerator."

"I'll be fast."

"Take your time."

"Okay, back in ten."

He turned and crossed the hall to his room and turned to close the door. Analise was leaning back against the butcher's block, watching. He intended to close the door, to head to the shower. To his surprise, his body propelled him back the way he'd come.

Three seconds later, Riley had one hand behind her head and the other wrapped behind her to pull her to him. One of her arms snaked around his body, fingers digging for purchase in his damp work-shirt as their lips met.

All thoughts of showering, having that beer or eating dinner fled. He couldn't think of anything, all he could do was feel her lush body pressing against his, her mouth taking as much as it gave and the little sound in her throat when his hand moved lower to cup the side of her rear.

Both of them jumped at the sudden pounding on the front door. They looked at one another and then in the direction of the front room. Riley opened his mouth to speak then closed it and headed for the door.

Bobby Daniels stood at the door, shifting weight from one foot to the other. "Mr. Riley, we got trouble."

Bobby's words made Riley's gut clench. "What kind of trouble?"

"Old Tom said he just heard on the news. Dust storm headed right for us and we got horses out in the pasture and the new calves out there as well."

Riley considered it for half a second. The cattle should be able to survive, unless the storm was too strong. The horses would panic and that could cost them stock, particularly the new foals "Have the hands saddle up. We'll round up the horses. With luck we'll get them in the barns before the storm hits. Tell Tom to pick three men to get everything secured. I'll meet you at the barn."

He closed the door to find Analise standing behind him holding his boots. "I can help."

"I know Cody taught you to ride, Annie but—"

"I can help. Please."

"Okay, grab two of my jackets from the closet in the laundry room and a couple of bandanas."

Analise hurried off to follow his instructions and Riley took a seat to pull on his boots. Dust storms were no joke in these parts. Big enough and they could rip roofs off buildings, flip vehicles and kill livestock.

A split second later the warning siren three miles away went off. They didn't have long. Analise ran back into the room, handing him a coat and a bandana. She wore one of his coats, the arms rolled up in a big wad around her wrists and the hem brushing her knees.

"Come on." He led the way.

Together they ran from the house and into the stable where the hands already had his horse saddled. He gestured to one of the senior hands, Russ Courtney. "Take Miss Annie to Tom and tell him she's here to help. Annie, as we get the animals you help Tom get them settled."

She nodded and he climbed on his horse. "We don't have long so let's get'r dun boys."

With a nod to Annie he kicked his horse into action. She watched Riley and his men ride away and then turned to Russ Courtney. "Show me what to do."

"Come with me."

Annie followed him to the bunkhouse where an older bearded gray-haired man was barking directions at three other men. "Boss said Miss Annie is here to help you, Tom."

The older man turned. "Tom Cleardon, ma'am. 'Preciate the help."

"Just tell me what to do."

For the next half hour it was a race to get everything moved into barns, to shutter windows on the bunkhouse and main house and tie down anything that couldn't be moved inside a structure. By the time an hour had passed the ranch hands were returning, driving horses in front of them.

Analise had never heard anything like this storm. It was like a train approaching, a roar that grew steadily louder. Thumps from debris hitting the barn and groans from the wood had her nerves stretched thin. With the whinnies of nervous horses, the wind and the shouts of men to one another it was bedlam.

After that Annie lost track of time. The roar of wind continued to grow stronger and before long flying debris slammed into the barn like gunshots. More of the men returned and she watched as they entered the barn and then as several men worked to close the doors and dropped a bar in place to secure them. She looked around. Where was Riley?

She saw Bobby and ran over to him. "Where's Riley?"

"Still out there. He was chasing a colt. He sent me back."

"He's still out there?" She tried not to jump as the lights flickered, but found herself reaching for Bobby's arm when they died.

"Get the generators going!" Tom's gravely voice rang out. "And close it all down."

"No!" She ran in the direction of his voice. "Someone has to find Riley."

"Can't. Storm's on us. Just gotta ride it out."

"No! You can't leave him—"

Tom grabbed her by the shoulders. "He knows what to do."

"No." She tore away from him. "If you won't send someone, I'll go."

She raced toward one of the horses that was still saddled. As she scrambled to get into the saddle someone grabbed her around the waist and pulled her off. Analise kicked and screamed but she couldn't get away. Finally she was released and she whirled to face Russ Courtney. "He could die out there!

"He won't die, Miss Annie. You just gotta have some faith. Riley knows what to do."

Have some faith? Right now it was taking all she had not to lose it and become a red hot mess of screaming and crying. She clenched her teeth so hard her jaws hurt and nodded. Russ gave her a pat on the shoulder and got back to the business at hand.

Analise looked around at everyone, all working toward a common goal and it hit her. They all believed without question that Riley would be okay. They were doing what he'd told them to do, protecting his place and his animals and none of them had any doubt that they would all survive the storm.

She wanted that faith. She needed it. It had taken a lifetime to find Riley Morgan and she couldn't lose him now.

Chapter Thirteen

Riley could taste dirt. Little wonder. The storm had been sizeable. As he rode, he surveyed what he could see of his land in the darkness. A couple of fences would need mending, and several trees had been pushed over. The oldest of the two barns was missing some roofing but all things considered things didn't look too bad.

This wasn't his first dust storm, but something had been different about this one. When he sent the rest of the men back, he figured he had time to get that colt and make it back before he got caught in the storm.

When he realized he'd miscalculated, he did the only thing he could do. Found as high a ground as possible, made the horse and the foal lie down and wedged himself between them with his coat covering him.

It didn't last long, though it seemed to stretch on forever and in those minutes Riley fully realized something that had changed everything. He wanted Annie. Not just for passion, but wanted her in his life. He'd known and liked her for a year and meeting her, and spending time with her had shown him that he did more than like her. He was in love with her.

He'd wasted a lot of his life chasing the wrong goals and the wrong women and now he wanted something real and solid. A home. With Annie.

He dismounted in front of the barn and pounded on the door. "Everyone all right in there?"

A few seconds he heard Annie's voice. "It's Riley. Open the door!"

The door opened and she flew out, launching herself at him. He caught her in midair and she wrapped her arms around his neck and her legs around his waist. Before he could catch his breath her lips were on his.

Riley forgot the taste of dirt and his bone-tiredness. Had it not been for the sudden chorus of cheers and hoots, he might have lost himself in that kiss. Annie pulled back and put her hands on his face. "Are you okay? Are you hurt?"

"I'm fine, honey."

She slid down him to get her feet beneath her. "I was so scared –"

"I'm fine." He looked at everyone. "Ya'll did a fine job and I'm in your debt. Now get some sleep. We'll have plenty to do at daylight."

Men filed out, clapping Riley on the shoulder or bidding him goodnight. He waited until they'd left then looped his arm over Annie's shoulders. "I'm so hungry I could eat the south end of a north bound mule right now."

"I can warm up dinner. Hopefully it's still okay."

"Sounds good to me."

Together they made their way to the house. Aside from scattered tree branches and a few fence posts, the front yard looked okay. Riley bypassed the front door and walked around to the back. He pulled off his boots and coat and tossed them into the laundry room as they entered.

"I gotta get clean. And pardon a man for saying, but you smell a little of horse, honey."

Analise looked up from pulling off her boots and grinned. "Then I guess I better head upstairs and get clean, too. Let me just turn on the oven to get things warmed up."

Riley followed her to the kitchen and watched as she checked the meal that was in the oven and turned it on. When she finished she turned to leave the room, he blocked her way.

"I thought—"

"I know." He took her hand and led her across the hall, through his bedroom and into the bathroom.

He reached into the shower to turn on the water and then turned to face her.

"Riley."

There it was again, two syllables that undid him, obliterated all other thought but wanting her. He reached for her and she met him, working her arms up around his neck. Her fingers tightened in his hair as her breasts crushed against his chest. Their mouths met in a clash of lips and tongues.

That initial collision of bodies only held them still for an instant. They two-stepped back against the wall and thudded against it in a tangle of limbs. Analise reached for purchase as Riley pinned her against the wall. Her hand found a towel rack and ended up pulling the towels from where they hung.

He heard her groan right before she grabbed his arms, fingers digging in as she tried to turn him against the wall. Her foot slid on a towel that had slid to the floor and she would have fallen as well had he not wrapped his arms around her and backed her over to the vanity.

Riley's hands went to work on the button of her jeans as she started tearing at his. His pants fell to his knees before he peeled hers off. He lifted her up onto the vanity counter and she wound her legs around him. He reached between them and angled a bit. One push and he was sliding into her wet sex.

Analise gasped at the initial penetration and then again as he picked her up, turned and pinned her against the wall. One curl of his pelvis and she moaned in pleasure. "Yes, please."

Then he took her. It was lust, hungry and primal but flavored with the intensity of love. She took and gave, exulting in the overwhelming sensations and the satisfaction he gave her time and time again. The third time she went into free-fall she felt his pulse heavy inside her. His body went rigid at the onset of his orgasm and she went with him.

When it ended, they were both sweaty and breathing hard. Riley slowly lowered her so that she could put her feet on the floor.

"I didn't mean – what I mean is I didn't intend – I wanted to do that a little slower."

"I didn't."

His look of surprise had her smiling. "We'll go slow next time."

"So there's going to be a next time?"

"Well, I guess that's up to you isn't it?" Suddenly she felt insecure. Would he toss her aside now? "I mean if it's just a one time—"

His kiss silenced her. "I want to love you slow and sweet, Annie. Often and repeatedly, but right now if I don't get clean and get something in my belly I think my stomach's gonna gnaw on my backbone."

"Then get in the shower, stud."

"Stud?"

She smiled, overcoming the moment of insecurity and stripped off the rest of her clothes. When she removed her bra he grinned. "Well, hello there my beauties."

With a laugh she scooted by him and got into the shower. A moment later he followed. It took a bit longer than normal to get clean since he seemed to be fixated on her breasts but eventually they finished. Analise dried off and wrapped a towel around her body. "I have to run upstairs and get some clothes."

"Grab a shirt from my closet."

"A shirt? I'm going to have dinner in just a shirt?"

"If I'm lucky."

She grinned and went into the bedroom. Inside his closet she found a soft cotton shirt. She had to roll the cuffs up several times because the sleeves were so long. It covered her from neck to upper thigh. She turned as he walked into the bedroom.

"Now that's the way to wear a shirt." He grinned and went to the chest of drawers to pull out a pair of soft cotton drawstring pants. He pulled out a t-shirt but she snatched it away from him.

"I like it better without the shirt."

"Whatever you want, honey. Now about that dinner...?"

They went into the kitchen and Analise got busy getting plates filled. Once done, they took their plates into the dining room.

Riley took one bite of the pot-roast and groaned. "Oh my god, this is good."

She grinned and they both dug in. Conversation was sparse and what was of it was about the storm. Analise was so caught up in thinking about what had just happened between them that she had a hard time following the conversation. She'd just had sex with Riley. And it was amazing.

Whoever said fantasy was better than reality was full of crap. She'd fantasized about Nate Bridges for years and never had her dreams been as good as what she'd just experienced. He didn't seem to mind periods of silence which was good for her. She wasn't quite sure what to talk about once they'd covered the storm topic.

When they finished, Riley helped her clean up the kitchen and put the leftovers away. He grabbed a beer and she poured a glass of wine and they took their drinks into the den.

Riley lit the fire, turned out the lights and they settled on the couch with Analise snuggled up next to him. Neither of them had much to say and that was fine with her. She was full, tired, had enjoyed several amazing orgasms and was feeling rather lazy.

"You tired, honey?" he asked as he put his empty bottle on the end table.

"A bit."

"Ready to turn in?"

"Are you?"

"Yeah, I think so. There'll be a lot to do tomorrow."

"Okay." She stood, picked up her empty wine glass and his beer bottle. He followed her to the kitchen and waited as she put the bottle into the trash and washed the glass.

"Well, I guess that's it." She walked over to him. "Good night, Riley." She stood up on tiptoes, kissed him softly and then started to skirt around him to head upstairs.

"Hold on there, Wildcat." He grabbed her hand and stopped her. "Stay with me, Annie."

Those words were the perfect end to the perfect fantasy. "If that's what you want."

"More than anything."

"Okay."

He led her into his room and turned back the bed. He slid off his pants and climbed in. Analise hesitated for a brief moment then took off the shirt and got in beside him. Riley turned off the lamp beside the bed and lay on his back, pulling her to his side. Analise put her head on his shoulder and draped her arm over him.

"I was wrong, Annie." His whisper was so low she almost didn't catch the words.

"About what?"

"I'm not falling in love with you."

Her world was a split second from crumbling beneath her when he continued. "I'm not falling, I'm already there, honey."

She almost cried, so much emotion filled her. It was more than a fantasy. It was a dream come true.

"I love you, Riley."

She felt his lips against her forehead and his arm tighten around her. "I love you. Good night, sweetheart."

And for the first night in a very long time, she fell asleep dreaming not of a fictional character or a movie idol but the very real man lying next to her.

Chapter Fourteen

Were it not for the nagging fear over Rick's predicament and possible threats to her son, Analise would label her days as perfect. There had been no trouble aside from the dust storm since she'd been at Riley's, and this morning when she spoke with David, he was going on a hundred miles an hour about the agents escorting him to Texas.

It was such a relief to know that he was safe, and she was looking forward to seeing him in two days. Until then, she was going to enjoy every moment she had with Riley. It was almost like being on a honeymoon. Well, aside from the mountain of work that had to be done on the ranch. She'd never realized ranch people worked so hard. Or had such a good attitude about it.

Riley wasn't a boss who just gave orders and stood back to watch everyone else work. No indeed. He labored as anyone else on the ranch. He did take some time in the evenings to work in his shop and she'd been thrilled to start helping him.

It was such a comfortable and companionable time. She asked a million questions and he answered every one patiently. She was learning so much and finding that she really enjoyed the woodworking.

Today he'd let her help with the birth of a foal. The baby was breach and she actually got to turn the creature inside its mother and help it into the world. It was amazing and she'd been full of energy all day. She'd done laundry, cleaned, written pages of notes and had finished in time to start dinner and take a shower.

She planned on having everything ready for when Riley walked through the door. She hummed as she stepped out of the shower and dried herself. When she started to wrap the towel around her body Riley walked into the bathroom, grabbed the towel, tossed it aside and captured her for along long wet kiss.

"Oh my god, you're good at that." Her voice was soft against his lips.

He grinned and waltzed her backward into the bedroom. "We're just getting started, honey."

She forgot about everything else but him and the pleasures they shared.. When at last their passion was sated, he lowered himself down on her, rolling over with his arms locked around her so that she lay against his side. With her head on his chest, Analise closed her eyes, listening to the rapid beat of his heart and feeling her own breath trying to return to normal.

For a long time he held her there then drew back and looked into her eyes. "You make me feel like a kid again."

She laughed. "Oh god, I don't think I could have handled you as a kid, Riley Morgan."

"No?"

"Well, I would've given it my best shot, you know, but seriously, don't even ask me to stand right now."

"Well damn, and here I was going to ask about dinner."

She pinched him lightly. "Oh so that's how this goes, eh?'

"Honey you gotta feed me if I'm gonna be doing all this world-class lovin'."

Analise laughed again. "Well, when you put it that way, let's get ourselves to the kitchen. It just so happens, I have a world- class dinner ready in the oven."

"World- class?"

"You better believe it, big guy."

She started to roll away but he stopped her and when she looked at him his expression was somber. "Annie, all kidding aside, I don't expect you to wait on me. I was just kidding about—"

"Riley, I like doing this for you. I like helping on the ranch and working in the shop. I even like taking care of the house and cooking. And I especially like doing it for you. It makes me happy."

"You sure?"

"Positive."

"I like you being here, Annie. It feels like – it feels like how I always wanted life to be."

"Me too."

"So…" he reached up to stroked her side of her face. "So, maybe we could make it a permanent thing?."

"What do you mean? I'm still married you know."

"Yeah, I know. But you could still live here. With me. And once you're divorced, if it's what you want we can—"

"Don't say it." She put her finger to his mouth. "Please. I want to be here with you. More than anything. But I don't want promises of marriage. To be honest, I don't know if that's a bridge I ever want to cross again. But we don't need a piece of paper, Riley. What I feel for you is stronger than that. I'm yours for as long as you want me."

"What if that's forever?."

"Forever sounds real good to me."

The kiss he gave her was the sweetest she'd ever received. She could feel his love and it flowed into her like warm light. When it ended she smiled at him. "Now, about that dinner?"

"Right behind you, ma'am." He rolled out of the bed and headed for the shower. "Soon as I clean up."

Analise smiled and watched him go. If only life could be like this every day.

Chapter Fifteen

Rodrick checked his rearview mirror again. It had taken far longer than he anticipated to lose the companion Moretti assigned to accompany him. The man was a bulldog, sticking to him to the point that Rodrick could barely take a piss without the man standing guard on the door.

It was in San Antonio that he'd finally managed to ditch the man. He insisted on going to a bar on Saturday night, and one that he wouldn't have frequented had desperation not demanded it. He'd even gone shopping for the night out.

Dressed in wrangler jeans, a plaid shirt, boots and a cowboy hat he purchased at a second hand store, he'd walked into walked into the country western bar at half past eleven at night. His companion, Tony, stuck out in his Italian suit and loafers, clearly identifying himself as an outsider.

Half the people there were well on their way to being drunk so it wasn't all that hard for him to start a brawl.He'd simply yelled at his companion. "Don't you fucking talk that way about Texas!"

Within thirty seconds the trouble started. Within two minutes, a fist fight ensued and within three, Rodrick was running out of the bar. He hailed a cab and asked to be taken to the hotel where they'd rented a room for the night. Five minutes later, he was packed and waiting on another cab to take him to a car rental place.

Now he was a good hundred miles from San Antonio with a rental car, a prepaid phone and a chance to get to Analise and talk her out of the money she'd taken before that psycho Moretti found him. If he could get his hands on the money, he fully intended to leave the country.

He'd spoken with someone his family did business with, a less-than-honest businessman who said he could get Rodrick to Mexico for ten thousand dollars. For another fifteen he could get Rodrick to a country with no extradition treaty with the States.

With the money Rodrick could get from Analise, he could live like a king for the rest of his life. So what that he left Gina behind? She'd certainly proven her loyalty was to her father and not to him. This was a time to think of saving himself and that was what he fully intended to do. All he had to do was find Analise. If Moretti was correct and she was in a little backwater town called Cotton Creek it should be easy. There couldn't be that many out-of-towners in a place like that, and greasing palms was a sure way to find out her location.

Satisfied that soon he would be a free man, he hummed to himself as he headed southwest.

*****

Analise ran down the steps of the front porch and across the front yard as David stepped out of the back of the black SUV. She threw her arms around him. "I'm so glad to see you."

"Me too." He returned the hug but was the first to pull away. "This is--wow, it looks like a real ranch."

"It is." She smiled at him and then turned to look at the tall man who climbed out of the driver's door of the SUV.

"Mrs. Becke? I'm Kade Lawson."

"It's a pleasure to meet you. And thank you so much."

He nodded then turned with a big smile as Riley's voice boomed out. "Kade Lawson."

"Riley."

They shook hands and Riley clapped him on the shoulder. "Appreciate you doing this, Kade."

"Happy to help. Oh, Riley, Mrs. Becke –" he gestured toward the beautiful brunette woman who was walking around the front of the SUV toward them. "My partner. Cia Whitehorse."

"Partner and wife," Cia said and stuck out her hand to Riley. "I've heard a lot about you. And while Kade told me you don't particularly like hearing it, I really enjoyed your movies. Shame you aren't doing that anymore."

"Mrs—" Riley was cut off by Cia.

"Cia. Please."

"Cia. Nice to meet you. And my thanks to you as well."

"Glad to help." She looked at Analise. "And this must be David's mom. Analise?"

Analise stuck out her hand. "I don't know how to thank you. Both of you. Knowing that David was safe – it – thank you. Thank you."

"You're welcome. And he's a great kid. Curious as a bag of cats but great."

Analise smiled. "I have lunch if you're hungry."

"I could eat." Kade replied.

"You can always eat." Cia teased.

"Then come on in." Riley gestured toward the house.

Analise hung back and walked with David. "You okay?"

"I'm not a kid, mom."

"I know that, but this is – this is not an ordinary situation."

"You mean about Dad turning out to be a thief and playing with mob money?"

Analise stopped in her tracks. "David, we don't know."

"Yeah, we do. At least the FBI does. Mom, he's in a world of shit and he's either going to go to jail or getting killed, depending on who finds him first."

"What do you mean depending on who finds him?"

"I overheard Kade and Cia talking. They thought I was asleep. He vanished a couple of days ago. That mobster has people out looking for him and the FBI has him on a no-fly list. So like I said—"

"I know, jail or getting killed."

"And before you say anything, I don't want that money. Not if he got it illegally."

"I'm proud of you for feeling that way, and I agree. I'll give it to the FBI or whatever they tell me to do. And I have enough – enough legally to help you out. I promised I'd support you until you were finished with school and that's what I'll do."

"I know you will. Never doubted it, Mom, but if I have to I can get financial aid and loans."

"But I don't want you to do that."

"But I will if I have to."

"Okay. Let's cross that bridge when we get to it. For the moment I'm just happy you're here and safe."

"I'm glad to see you but …"

When his gaze slid away she took hold of his arm. "What is it?"

"This guy, Riley. He's your friend, right? The one you've been going on about for the last year?"

"Yes."

"Just a friend?"

Analise had never out-and-out lied to her son and she wasn't going to start now. "No, he's more than that."

"You love him?"

"Yes. I do."

"And you want to stay here with him?"

"Very much."

David shrugged. "Well, if Kade's right then I guess Riley's a pretty stand-up guy. You do know he used to be an actor, right?"

"Yeah, that was a shocker."

"But he's a good man, isn't he?"

"The best."

"Well he better be if he wants my Mom. Otherwise, I might have to break out my mad ninja skills."

Analise laughed. "I don't think that will be necessary but I do appreciate you having my back."

"Always."

"Same here."

David gave her a hug then released her. "So what'd you fix to eat?"

"Steak sandwiches, potato salad, baked beans and an apple pie."

"I'm down with that."

"Then let's get to it."

Lunch passed in an easy atmosphere. Kade and Cia were interesting people, and seemed to be wildly in love. It was easy to tell from the looks they shared. Kade told about being assigned to guard Riley when he was in Dallas on a film and all the trouble they got into.

Everyone laughed at the tale, including Riley. They were just finishing dessert, when Bobby Daniels rapped at the front door. Riley got up to answer it.

"What's up Bobby?"

"That new mare? We're about to unload her and I figured you'd wanna be there."

"Yeah, I do. Let me grab my hat."

He walked back into the dining room. "Got a new mare that just came in and I need to be there when they unload her. Get her settled in. Moving sometimes gets 'em disconcerted."

"A horse?" David asked.

"Yes. Nice little paint I got for your mama."

"For mom?" He looked at Analise. "You can ride?"

"I can now."

"Can I go see?" He directed the question to Riley.

"Sure. Come on. Kade, you and Cia gonna be around a while?"

"Only long enough to go over some things with Analise then we're headed back to the field office to bring everyone here up to speed before we leave for DC."

"Well if I'm not back, stop by the paddock on your way out."

"Will do."

"Okay, young buck, let's do it." Riley said to David.

"You mind?" David asked Analise.

"Not at all."

"Thanks. And thanks Mr. Lawson and Mrs. Whitehorse. I appreciate everything you've done for me and my mother and I'm serious about what I said before. If you can put in a good word for me..."

"Consider it done." Kade got up to shake David's hand and Cia rose to give him a kiss on the cheek.

"You take care, Dave." She said and smiled.

"You too. Okay, I'm ready."

He left with Riley. Kade and Cia reclaimed their seats. Analise looked from one to the other. "Before we get started, can I ask you something?"

"Sure." Kade mumbled around his last bite of pie.

"Who's the guy in the plaid shirt?"

Kade literally spewed. Cia grabbed a napkin and started wiping at the mess as Kade caught his breath. "What guy?"

"That one." Analise pointed across the table towards an older man with long gray hair pulled back in a ponytail, and wearing a plaid shirt.

"You see a man sitting there?" Cia asked.

"Well of course she does, Gracie." The man said in a decidedly Southern accent then smiled at Analise. "I'm Joe."

"Nice to meet you, Joe. I'm Anali—Annie."

"Annie suits you."

"Yeah, I think it does too. So, tell me. Why didn't Riley and David notice you were here?"

"David knows I'm here. He can see me. Not everyone can."

"And why is that?"

Joe shrugged and then looked at the pie. "Mind?"

"Help yourself." She got up to get him a plate and silverware. "Would you like some sweet tea?"

"I surely would."

Analise got him a glass of tea and then sat back down at the table. "Okay, I'm really trying not to freak out here, but I get the feeling you people are not the run-of-the-mill FBI agents, so can we all put our cards on the table?"

"Amen to that." Cia agreed. "Kade and I work for a special division of the FBI, the SACU or Specialized Anomalous Crime Unit. We typically investigate any crime in which paranormal activity is suspected."

"Paranormal? So, what are you, psychics?"

"Not all, but all do have paranormal abilities."

"Such as?"

"We have a telepath capable of communication with humans or animals, an empath who senses the physical and emotional states of others, agents who are precognitive, one skilled in retrocognition, clairvoyants, clairaudients, a clairsentient and those who have psychometric abilities. We also have people skilled in remote viewing, aura vision, one of our agents can astral project and we have two mediums."

"And you?"

"I see the dead."

Analise gestured toward Joe. "Is he dead?"

"No."

"Then what is he?"

"An angel." Kade said, then quickly added. "For lack of a better word."

"An angel." Analise looked at Joe and smiled. "Well, I could use an angel right about now."

Kade and Cia looked at one another and then at Analise. "You don't seem surprised or disturbed about what Cia just told you." Kade remarked.

Analise smiled again. "I was born in the mountains of Georgia, just a small little place populated by decent hard-working folks, including some who would have been shunned by mainstream society. My maternal grandmother was one of those. A witch."

"Wiccan?" Cia asked.

"No. She just had abilities, some of which you mentioned."

"Did you inherit any of her abilities?"

"I didn't think so – until now. Grannie could – see things. People no one else could see. So, while there's part of me that feels like the kid who wants to go hide under the bed, another part accepts it as something in the realm of possible.

"But that's not why we're all here and I'm sorry I sidetracked you. I wanted you to know upfront that I did take money from offshore accounts that my husband has. I put it all into a trust for David. I also took money from joint accounts we shared. I have those funds and I'm willing to bet they're legal. Rodrick would not have put the money in US banks if they weren't.

"I'll dissolve the trust and return the money if that's what's necessary. I only took it so that David would be provided for. He could finish school, start his life and not have to worry."

"We appreciate that, Analise." Kade looked at Cia for a moment and then continued. "However, at the moment our primary objective is locating your husband. If we can get him to testify to money laundering for organized crime, we may have a foothold to put Moretti and more like him away."

"Will Rodrick go to prison?"

"That depends upon the depth of his involvement. Like I said, first we have to find him. We suspect he will either be trying to flee the country, or come here and try to get the money back from you. That's why Joe is going to look in on you while we're gone."

"You're staying here?" Analise looked at Joe.

"Naw, just gonna pop in now and then to make sure everything's okay."

"Oh, okay. So what do you want me to do?"

"Just let us know if you hear from your husband." Cia answered the question and slid a card across the table to Analise. "Call my cell anytime."

"Thank you. Again. I appreciate everything you're doing."

"You're welcome, but I'm afraid we're not quite done. We need to ask you some questions, Analise. About your husband's business and your knowledge of it."

"Okay. I don't know anything since I was never a part of it but ask away."

"She doesn't know anything, Gracie." Joe spoke up.

Cia cut him a look and they stared at one another for a moment. "I still have to ask, Joe."

"Have it your way." He went back to eating pie.

Cia activated the video app on her phone and turned it toward herself. After stating her name, Kade's presence and the date, she put the phone on the table, pointed at Analise.

"Mrs. Becke. Please state your name for the record.

With a sigh, Analise did as instructed, her thoughts not as much on the questions as on David out in the paddock with Riley.

*****

Riley walked the mare around the paddock then slipped off the bridle and walked away from her. It took a couple of seconds before she followed. He smiled to himself as he walked over to the fence where David and Bobby sat on the top rail with the man he'd bought the horse from, JD Weathers.]

Riley had always thought that JD was the one who should have gone to Hollywood. If ever a man looked the role of a western hero it was JD, or Justice Weathers. Tall and big, he had a hard look to him, with flinty eyes and a face of angles that made him appear a little dangerous.

He would have turned the heads of a whole lot of those Hollywood women. But JD wasn't a man given to fanciful or superficial things. He was a down-to-earth rancher with a family to take care of and that seemed to be his only focus in life.

"She's a beauty, Mr. Riley." Bobby said.

"Yep, she is."

"So you really got it for my mother?" David asked.

"Yep. That okay with you, David?"

"Yeah, I guess."

"Good. JD, I appreciate you bringing her over." Riley pulled a check out of his top shirt pocket.

"No problem. She's a sweet thing. I think your gal's gonna like her."

Riley put his hand on JD's shoulder and turned him away from the fence, talking to the boys as he did. "I'm gonna speak with JD for a few. I'll be back."

"Take your time, boss." Bobby grinned and immediately started talking to David.

"So, how's the family, JD?" Riley asked as they walked toward JD's truck.

"Good."

"Those boys of yours are on fire this year. I missed the last couple of games, but keep up with it through Cody and her family. Team's leading the division, I hear."

"Yeah, they're having a hell of a year."

"Frank down at the feed store mentioned that they were being scouted pretty heavily."

JD smiled. "Yeah and loving it."

"As they should. They have their eyes on a school?"

"A couple. UT in Austin is courting them pretty strong and I thought they were going to commit, but then Notre Dame and Ohio State started wooing them."

"They offering full rides for the boys?"

"I wish. They're offering some but god almighty what it leaves owing more than I can wrap my head around."

"You know I'll help if I can. I'm happy to pitch in if it helps them get where they want to go."

"I appreciate that Riley. You're a good friend. The problem as I see it is they don't really know what they want – outside of playing football that is. They've got those pie-in-the-sky dreams of making the big league and we all know how slim those chances are. They're my boys and I'm proud of them. They're good players, but the truth is there are a lot of good high school players. Few of them wind up playing pro."

"It's not necessarily wrong to follow a dream."

"No, but you've gotta be realistic. Go to college and learn something."

"So you can leave the farm? You stayed home and you've done alright for yourself and your boys."

JD shrugged. "I'm not complaining. Ranching is all I know aside from rodeoing and the rodeo days are way behind me. I just want better for my boys."

"You're a good man, JD."

"I don't know so much about that." JD started closing up the trailer.

"How's your brothers' construction business?"

"Holding its own but not making us rich."

"They sure did a good job on the renovations on my place."

"Yeah, they do good work."

"Indeed they do. Well, I best get back to the boys. Thanks again."

"You bet. Take care, Riley."

"You too."

Riley made his way back to the boys and looked at Bobby. "Bobby how 'bout giving me and David a minute."

"Sure, Boss." Bobby swung his leg over the rail, hopped down and then turned to look at David. "If you're interested in going let me know. I'll head out after work. Around seven."

"Thanks. I am. Swing by and I'll be ready."

"You got it."

"You and Bobby have plans?" Riley wasn't surprised that Bobby was being friendly. It was his nature.

"Yeah. He said he wanted to take me over to Billy's, wherever that is. Said they have the world's best barbecue and really pretty girls working there."

"Well, yes they do – on both counts, but heads up on the girls. Any girl with a last name of Sweet, you'll want to tread carefully. Their daddy owns the bar."

"Good to know. Thanks. So, I'm assuming you sent Bobby away because you have something to say to me."

"I do."

"Okay."

"I want you to know that I care deeply about your mother and I'll do everything in my power to make sure she's safe – while this thing with your father is going on and when it's done."

"Are you in love with my mother, Mr. Morgan?."

"Riley. And yes I am."

David looked at him for several long seconds. "I read up on you during the trip. I know you were a huge film star at one time, and I know you've been married and divorced multiple times. There's little information about you after you left Hollywood, so I want to know. Have you been married again since you've been here?"

"No."

"So there are the three divorces and that's it?"

"Yes."

"And do you plan on my mother being your fourth wife?"

Riley reached up and scratched his chin. "Well, we haven't quite gotten that far along, David."

"So maybe you won't want to marry her. Maybe you just want to shack up with her for a while until you get tired of her, And what then? I don't know you at all, Mr. Morgan, aside from what my mother's told me, but I do know her. She's not the kind of person to just take up with a man for a fling. And I don't think she'd want someone to take up with her if that's their reasoning."

Riley smiled. He couldn't be offended by what David said, because he was doing what any son who loved his mother would do. He was vetting Riley to see if Riley measured up. "I agree with you completely, David. About your mom, I mean. She's a special woman, and I'd never treat her as anything less."

David nodded and stuck out his hand. "I'm going to take your word on that, Mr. Morgan, but make no mistake. You hurt my mom and you *will* answer to me."

"I'd expect no less." Riley clasped David's hand and gave it a firm shake. "Now, what say we get back to the house and see if your mother is finished with the questions Kade had for her."

"Sounds good."

As they walked back to the house, Riley asked David about his life, what he enjoyed and what he wanted out of life. The answers he received made him think David was a young man with a good head on his shoulders. Obviously, he'd had a good upbringing and Riley was willing to bet that was due to Analise.

She, Kade and Cia were just walking out of the house when he and David reached the yard. "Ya'll all set?"

"Yep." Kade walked down the steps and extended his hand to Riley. "Hope to see you again soon, old friend. Under different circumstances."

"Likewise, Kade. My home's always open so any time you and Cia want a place to hang your hat in Texas, you know where to kick off your boots."

"I'm gonna take you up on that."

"I hope so." Riley stuck out his hand to Cia as she walked up beside Kade. "You keep him in line, Cia and take care."

"Oh I will. And you too. Riley. If anything, and I mean anything, out of the ordinary happens, get in touch with Kade or me immediately. We have someone in the area keeping an eye on things, but want to know if anything looks out of the ordinary."

"Yes ma'am."

"Then I guess we'll get out of your hair."

"Safe journey."

Cia looked at David. "You'll be hearing from us soon, Dave. Keep your eyes and ears open and if—"

"You'll hear from me if anything looks suspicious."

"Good man." She looked back over her shoulder at Annie who was standing behind her. "Talk to you soon, Annie."

"I hope so. Be safe."

"Gonna try." She looked up at Kade. "Okay, big guy, let's hit the road."

With a grin and a wave, they did just that. Everyone watched them leave except David. Riley noticed he was looking in the direction of the rocking chairs on the porch."Everything okay, David?"

"Huh? Oh yeah. Yeah. Great. Hey, Mom, I'm going to head out with Bobby later and go get some barbecue. That okay with you?"

"You're going out? I – well, do you think that's wise? I mean—"

"It'll be fine." He cut his eyes back to the porch for a split seconds. "Trust me, first sign of trouble and I'll be 911'ing like a speed demon."

She chuckled. "Fine. Until then, you want to get your things settled?"

"Sure."

She looked at Riley. "Which room?"

"The one at the front of the house upstairs is the biggest."

He saw the look of panic that came on her face and realized that she probably hadn't told David she was sleeping in his bed. Riley didn't believe in playing games or trying to hide anything. He wasn't ashamed of what he and Analise were doing.

"David, I need to be straight with you. Man to man."

David looked him in the eye and Riley could tell his words had a good deal of impact. He suspected it was the "man-to-man" part. "Your mother isn't just hiding out here. She's living with me – we're living together. I told you I'm in love with your mother and I don't say that lightly. But I want you to know upfront that she's not just sharing my house. She's sharing my bed."

David looked from Riley to Analise. "It's your life, Mom and your choice. If you're happy, then that's all that matters. I'm going to tell you just like I told Riley. As long as he's good to you and doesn't hurt you in any way, I don't have a problem.

"But I'm not going to see you become someone else's doormat. You put up with Dad's bullshit my entire life and I know it was because you thought you were doing it for me. But I don't want that for you anymore. You're smart and talented and should realize by now that you can make it on your own without depending on a man.

"I'm not saying you don't deserve someone in your life, just that you don't need them for survival. If Riley makes you happy then I hope it stays that way. If it does you won't get any shit from me."

Riley saw the tears that welled up in Analise's eyes. She didn't try to hide them. She just let them spill and smiled through them at her son. "When did you get to be so wise and aware?"

David smiled. "I had a good teacher."

"And an observant one." She said, which puzzled Riley, but apparently not David because he cut a look at Riley and then at the ground.

"We'll talk later, Mom. Right now, let's haul my stuff upstairs. I need to get online – oh hey, Riley do you have internet?"

"Why yes we do, along with running water and satellite."

David laughed. "Well hell, I guess this isn't quite Bumfuck, Texas after all."

"Oh it's Bumfuck," Riley said as he gestured towards the door. "Just a little less than what people imagine."

Analise smiled at him and he took her hand. It had been a somewhat tense day, with her being nervous about the arrival of her son and being questioned by the FBI, not to mention worrying that he and David might hit it off like oil and water.

So far, it had worked out and for that he was grateful. He'd be a lot more grateful when the FBI found Analise's husband and the mobsters he was involved with and made sure she was no longer in any danger. Until they did, he was going to make damn sure that nothing happened to her or David.

They might not be a married couple, but she was his woman, that was for damn sure. And anyone who tried to hurt her was going to have to come through him.

Chapter Sixteen

Rodrick cursed as he hurried back to the used car. He'd run into some bad luck in Midland. The fake identity he'd been assured would stand up to anything ended up belonging to someone with the credit rating of pond scum. The credit cards were, therefore, worthless, which meant he couldn't extend the duration of the rental car. Cash, apparently, was not accepted for such things.

His only option was to purchase a used car. A very cheap used car that, as it turned out, had no air conditioning, sounded like the vehicle equivalent of an asthmatic and had tires that had long since possessed tread.

But it was transportation and something he could afford to buy and ditch when the time came with no one the wiser that it was Rodrick Becke who'd purchased it.

He climbed into the wheezing compact, started the engine and set out to find a cheap place to stay for the night, hopefully one that accepted cash. He found one off the highway, a rundown motel that catered to "nightly" regulars.

Rodrick could care less what the people next door were doing. He took his plastic bag and his small travel case inside, locked the door and went straight to the bathroom. After disrobing, he read the instructions on the hair coloring.

Less than an hour later, his blond hair was gone. Now his needing- to- be- trimmed hair was the color of coal, as was the mustache and scraggly beard he had let grow since leaving New York. Not even his own father would recognize him, which was exactly what he wanted.

He dined on the cold burger and fries he'd picked up at a drive thru, downed the watery soda and stripped back the stained bedcover. At least the sheets appeared to be clean. He stretched out on the bed and turned on the television, scanning the news stations.

Ten minutes later he was sitting up as if he'd been stabbed in the back. Fear had his heart racing and sweat breaking out on his skin. Now not only was his father and brother in jail, but he was on the most wanted list. He grabbed the disposable phone and accessed the browser. His destination was nearly two hundred miles from his current location, if he was, in fact, headed for the right place. Cotton Creek, Texas

Tomorrow by this time, that's where he would be. And he would not leave until he had the money she'd taken from him. With that, and with the thumb-drive in his pocket containing the evidence that proved his brother Rolf was the mastermind behind the money laundering scheme, he could cut a deal and if lucky, walk away with the rest of the money that no one knew anything about.

Feeling calmer now that he'd thought things through and remembering that he was smarter than the FBI chasing him, as well as all of Moretii's henchmen, he turned the channel on the television to an old movie, lay back and let his mind go over each step of his plan.

*****

Analise let out a yelp as she was grabbed from behind. It only took a split second for her to realize who it was when Riley kissed the side of her neck. "Hmmm, eau de walnut."

She laughed and turned to face him. "I thought you weren't going to be back until dinnertime?"

"It is dinnertime."

"Are you serious?"

Riley laughed. "You get lost?"

"I guess so. But look. I got almost half-way around the table and it's not looking too bad."

Riley leaned over to study the table top she was working on. It was the table he was building for Billy to give to his wife, Stella. Analise had drawn a border around the outer perimeter of the table about a half an inch from the edge, and another closer to the center of the table, much smaller. It was engraved into the wood and inside that was a vine and what appeared to be roses, filling the border.

He'd seen the design when she drew it and thought it beautiful but he was doubtful she would be able to carve it with her little Dremel tool and make it look right. It appeared he was wrong.

"That's amazing, honey."

"Really?"

"Really. Billy and Stella are going to love this."

"I'm so happy that you let me help."

"I'm so happy you wanted to." He turned her back to face him and claimed a kiss. Her arms went around his neck and the kiss quickly heated up.

She pulled back and blew out her breath. "Damn, is it getting hot in here?"

"Just a bit."

She laughed. "Okay, since I've been a slack ass, I better get a move on. What do you want?"

Riley's answer was to reached behind her, grab her ass and pull her up against him. She gave another laugh. "Well, as tempting as that is, I fear we may have a revolt if I don't cook. David said he'd asked Bobby to join, if you don't mind."

"Not if you don't."

"No, not at all. I'm glad David has found a friend and I like Bobby."

"Did David tell you that he heard back from Cia?"

"No. About what?"

"About joining the FBI."

"Are you serious? I thought –"

"Apparently he does still intend to get his law degree, but according to Kade he wants to apply for the FBI once he passes the bar. He's talking to Cia and Kade about how to specialize to maximize his chances."

"Well damn, I feel like the last to know."

"He was planning on telling you, but he was a little worried about your reaction. He seems to think you expect him to graduate and be some big corporate attorney."

Analise gaped at Riley in shock. "What on earth made him think that?"

"Not a clue, but now you know so when he tells you, it won't pull the rug out from under you."

"Thanks for telling me. And we better get in and get cleaned up so I can start on dinner or I'm gonna have three ill-tempered men to deal with."

"How about we get clean and throw some steaks on the grill. We can wrap some potatoes up in foil and put them in the coals and all you have to do is chop up a salad and heat some bread."

"Now that sound good."

"Then let's do it, hot stuff."

She smiled, gave him a quick kiss and then together they headed for the house. Analise thought about David. It bothered her a little that he'd confided in Riley before her, but she told herself maybe Riley was a father figure for David. His own father had not shown much interest in him, and in the short time David had been here, he and Riley had gotten close.

That brought a smile to her face. "Oh, did I tell you that Cody asked me to help out at the bar during the after homecoming party?"

"No." Riley looked down at her. "Waiting tables?"

"And working the bar."

"You want to do that?"

"Yes, actually I do. You're going to be playing with the guys aren't you?"

"That's what I'm told."

"You don't mind if I help her out do you?"

"Not at all. In fact, I think it's real nice of you."

"You know, I love Cody. I know there's a difference in our ages, but she's become a good friend and I'm happy when I can help out her and her family. They're all such good people."

"Yeah, they are."

They walked in the house to find David and Bobby hard at work in the kitchen. "What's all this?" Analise looked around.

"We're cooking."

"You're cooking?"

"Well, sort of. I started the grill. Hope that's okay, Riley. And defrosted some steaks. Bobby's got potatoes all clean and in the coals and I'm making your homemade macaroni and cheese and a salad."

"Sounds good." Riley said. "And since you fellas have it all in hand, we're gonna go clean up." He took Analise's hand and tugged her in the direction of the hall. "Oh, hey, Bobby, will you check and make sure there's enough cold beer? Don't' know about you guys, but I could use a few. I have a case in the pantry you can throw in the ice bucket It's in the laundry room and there are bags of ice in the big freezer in there."

"On it, Boss!'

"Good man."

He tugged Analise across the hall and into his room, closed the door behind them and started peeling off his clothes. Analise followed suit and was just sliding out of her jeans when his phone rang. "Check to see who that is, will ya honey?"

She picked up his phone where he'd tossed it on the bed. "Holy shit." She handed him the phone. He took it, looked at the display and hit ignore.

"Riley! Didn't you read the caller ID?"

"Yep."

"And you're not curious what—"

"Nope."

"Really?" She finished undressing, took her dirty clothes to the hamper, then went into the bathroom and started the water in the shower.

"Nope."

"Why?"

"They or one of the other studios call every now and again, trying to get me to take a part."

"And you're done with acting?."

"Yep."

"You're not even a little bit tempted?"

"Nope."

She was secretly glad to hear him say that. Living here with him as Riley Morgan, in a place where everyone knew him and accepted him for the man he was and not the roles he'd played, was comfortable and safe and –normal. She was certain they wouldn't last if he went back to being Nate Bridges. There would be too much distraction, and too many women offering themselves to him.

Analise wasn't unsure of herself as a woman, but she knew she'd never be able to handle that. It would make her jealous and miserable.

"So, you have everything you want here?" She asked as she stepped into the shower and he stepped in behind her.

Riley took her in his arms. "I do now."

Funny how three little words had the power to make her so happy. Pushing him under the spray of water, she lifted her face for his kiss. For this moment, everything was right in her world and she was going to enjoy it.

By the time they were out of the shower and dressed, David and Bobby had dinner ready. They ate, listening to Bobby and David talk about David's exploits learning to ride and round up cattle. There was a lot of laughter and good natured teasing and for a little while she found herself imagining this was her life.

After dinner, she and Riley took care of the dishes and David and Bobby went into the den and turned on the television. Analise was just putting up the last of the dishes when she heard David's voice.

"Mom! Mom! Get in here!"

She and Riley ran into the den to see David pointing at the television. Analise took one look and felt all of the happiness of the day evaporate. The news report was about Rodrick's family business. An indictment had been handed down for money laundering, insider trading and a host of other things. They showed Rodrick's father and his brother, Rolf, handcuffed and being loaded into the back of police cars.

And then the report focused on Rodrick. A spokesperson for the FBI was shown. There was an active manhunt for Rodrick Becke.

When the newscast ended, Analise looked at David and then at Riley. He simply offered her his hand and led her to the couch. They took a seat and she looked at David again.

"He's in deep shit, mom."

"Yes."

"Are you okay?"

"Yes. No. I don't know. Are you?"

"Yes."

"Are you sure?"

"Yeah. He did this to himself mom. We had nothing to do with it and he never asked if we wanted to be part of it. He did it without considering what it might to do us and I hope they find him and lock him up."

"David you don't mean—"

"Yes, I do. Look, I know you taught me to respect him because he's my father, but the truth is, he gave me less attention than he did the dog."

"We didn't have a dog, honey."

"Exactly my point. I love you mom, but dad? I don't even know who he is except the man who disapproved of everything I ever did. Nothing was ever good enough. I was never good enough. He didn't care about me. I was no more to him than you – we were just window dressing, props he thought he needed to give the appearance of a stable married man with a family. A successful man, pillar of the community."

"David, your father does care—"

"Yeah, that's obvious isn't it? He cares so much that we've both been questioned by the FBI, are in danger from a bunch of mobsters and can't go home. What kind of caring is that?"

"I—" Suddenly she couldn't do it anymore. Couldn't make up excuses and try to spin Rodrick's behavior. "I agree. He doesn't care for either of us the way we would have wanted, and I'm sorry for that. I guess I thought I could care enough for both of us and if I didn't, I'm sorry. Really sorry.

221

"But he's not a bad man, David. He'd never intentionally hurt—"

"Mom stop it!" His voice rose in anger. "He might not be a murderer or drug dealer, but he took money from people who are. The money you put in my trust is money he stole from people like that. It's blood money and I want nothing to do with it – and nothing to do with him."

"I understand—"

"No." His voice lowered. "No, you don't, mom. You always look for the best in people and sometimes that makes you blind to who they really are because you're wanting so much for them to be who you want them to be. But he's not, mom. He never has been. He – he's been cheating on you for a long time."

"I know about that girl."

"She's not the first. He's had others."

That was news that both hurt and embarrassed her. She hated to have Riley and Bobby hearing all of the sordid details of her failed life. "Okay, he was a bad husband and a bad father. But we're away from him now and you never have to see him again if you don't want to. I just don't want what he's done to make you resentful or bitter. I don't want it to ruin—"

David bounded across the room and sat down beside her, pulling her into a hug. "He's not going to ruin my life. Or yours either." He pulled back, looked at her and then at Riley. "You have something good here, Mom. You have someone good here. Someone with honor. Hang onto that and be happy.

"I'm going to be happy. I spoke with Kade today. As soon as all of this is settled with my father, I'm going to apply to the FBI. Kade said if I am accepted, I can go through the training and they have special arrangements that can be made so I can go to law school and work. I can be part of the division he and Cia work with. I want to do that. I always wanted to make a difference and now I can."

"With the SACU?"

David nodded and she took his hand. "If that's what you want, then do it. You know I'll support you every step of the way."

"That I do. And now—" he got up, grabbed the remote and turned off the television. "Enough of that. What say we have a couple of beers and throw some darts? Bobby has a dart board at the bunk house."

"Why don't you men go ahead and do that? I'm kind of tired and I have a busy day tomorrow helping Cody get ready for the weekend homecoming thing."

"That's a pretty big deal around here isn't it?" Bobby asked.

"Oh yeah." Riley answered. "And I think I'll call it a day, too. You guys take as much of the beer as you want, but remember that in the morning we've got a good half a mile of fence to replace on the western border, and I expect you up and ready to go by six."

"We won't be late." Bobby said with a grin.

"If you're on time, you're late." David added.

"Okay, get out of here. Me and Annie need some quiet."

David gave Analise a kiss on the cheek, then he and Bobby headed to the kitchen. She heard them as they got their beer and left via the back door. Then she looked at Riley. "Well, the shit's hit the fan now, hasn't it?"

"Yep."

"Are you still sure you want us here, Riley?"

"Absolutely."

"I don't know why."

"Yes, you do."

She smiled and leaned over, snuggling up to his side. He wrapped his arm around her and kissed her forehead. "I like that boy of yours, Annie."

"I'm glad. I think it's good for him to be around you."

"Yeah?"

"Yeah."

"And is it good for you to be around me?"

"You have no idea how good."

"Then how about we make it permanent?"

She pushed away to look at him. "Meaning?"

"Meaning live here with me. I mean live, as in this is your home, too. Be mine and let me be yours."

"I notice you didn't say anything about marriage."

"Is that what you want?"

"No. I don't need a piece of paper, Riley. I know I love you. That's enough for me."

"Me too, honey. Me too."

Chapter Seventeen

Analise heard the sound of voices on the back porch. She saved the file she was working on, closed her laptop and placed it on the coffee table, then got up and went to the back door. Riley and David were sitting on the back steps talking.

She opened the door and walked out. "Hey guys. I wasn't expecting you for another hour."

Both men turned to look at her but only Riley smiled, a fact she took note of. "Everything okay?"

"Fine." Riley stood with his boots in one hand. "Just talking about all the homecoming doings that start tonight."

"That's it?"

Riley looked down at David and David shook his head. Riley blew out his breath. "Fine. I was going to wait until later to tell you."

"Tell me what?" A shard of fear had her tensing.

"Seems some eager beaver reporter figured out you were here, connected the dots and has been calling wanting Nate to make a statement on what he's doing shacked up with a mob wife on the run."

"A mob wife?" She looked at him and then at David. "A mob wife?"

"Well, Dad is wanted by the FBI and he's all over the news in the case they have against his family and their ties to organized crime."

"But a mob wife? Me? That's – that's the most ridiculous thing I ever heard. But—" she looked at Riley, "but I know you don't want your privacy invaded and I'm so sorry, Riley. Tell me what to do and I'll do it. If you want us to leave—"

"You're not going anywhere." He glanced down at David. "Either of you. I can handle the reporter. It's not my first rodeo, honey. It'll be okay. It's just an eager guy trying to land a story."

"Eager is an understatement," David commented. "The guy's been blowing up Riley's phone for the last three days."

That kind of hit Analise wrong. "Why didn't you mention it?"

"It didn't seem worth getting you upset."

"But you could confide in my son?"

"He heard me talking and asked. I wasn't going to lie. And I was going to tell you. I was just waiting for the right time."

Analise didn't want to make more of it than there was, so she let it go. "Okay. So, are you men excited about the big day? Cody says there's a parade after the game and then the high school is having a dance, and everyone else will he headed for the bar."

"Yep, I'm ready. In fact, I let everyone have the rest of the day and half the day tomorrow off."

"Well then get yourselves in the house and get cleaned up. I told Cody I'd catch up with her after the parade and help her get things set up in the bar. Oh, and her family wanted to know if we wanted to have an early dinner with them at the bar before the crowd arrives. Around five?"

"Fine by me." Riley looked at David. "Dave?"

"Works for me." David stood. "I'll head on up to the shower. I'm riding with Bobby, by the way, so you guys go on whenever you're ready. I'll see you at Billy's at five?"

"Yep. And invite Bobby." Riley said to David's back, and to Analise's questioning look added in a lower voice. "They like him and it'll be good for David to have a friend there. So, you upset with me Wildcat?"

"No. And I wasn't trying to start a fight, Riley. I guess it just hurt my feelings that you told David and didn't think you could tell me without upsetting me."

"Are you upset about it?"

"No. But then our situations aren't the same. For people to know that I'm here with you is no hardship at all. It's like being homecoming queen or the girl who dates the quarterback. Kind of exciting to be basking in the warmth of that star's shine."

"Honey, I'm no star."

She stepped over and looped her arms around his neck. "Riley Morgan, you'll always be a star to me."

"Riley or Nate?"

"Is there a difference? Now when I see you in a movie, I'll see Riley. Riley playing a role. Nate is just a name you used to use. Kind of the way I've been Analise my entire life, but now when I think of myself I think, Annie."

"Have I told you today that I love you?"

"Not nearly enough."

"I love you, Annie Becke."

"And I love you. Now go get clean so you can take me to town, cowboy."

"Yes ma'am. But first…"

The kiss had her nerves sizzling. Would he always have the power to excite her this way with a kiss?

She hoped so.

*****

Analise started waving the moment she spotted KC Sweet on the homecoming float. KC looked beautiful and was beaming. It wasn't every day a girl was crowned homecoming queen and Analise had no doubt that this would be one of the red-letter days of KC's life.

Once the float passed, she tugged on Riley's arm. "I'm going to head for the bar to help get everything ready."

"Want me to run you over there?"

"No. I'll ride with Cody. She's right down the block with Billy and Stella in front of the Sweet Shop."

"Okay, so I'll see you in a little while."

She stood up on tiptoe and kissed him. "See ya."

Analise started working her way through the crowd. It seemed like everyone in Cotton Creek was lining the street. She smiled and inched her way along, smiling and speaking to the few people she knew and smiling at those she didn't.

It took nearly ten minutes to cover half a block. Analise worked her way to the rear of the crowd and made her way to the end of the block as quickly as possible. There she made a left turn. She could cut through to the next street and make much better time.

The alleyway wasn't very wide, barely enough for one line of cars. When she made it to the end of the alley she started to make a right turn and was suddenly pulled back.

Some had a tight grip on her right arm and had put their other hand over her mouth.

Analise struggled against her captor but he was bigger and stronger, and twisted her arm up behind her. She was shoved along by her unknown assailant, led down the block to an old beat-up car, and then shoved against it.

She whirled around, intent on fighting. One look at her captor and she froze in shock. "Rick?"

Her husband looked at her through eyes set into hollow sockets. Dark bags beneath his eyes and more than a few days unshaven growth, combined with a really horrible black dye job to his hair gave him the look of a drug addict.

"What are you doing here?"

"Analise, we need to talk."

"We don't have anything to talk about. I filed for divorce."

"I'm in trouble. You've got to give me that money back."

"No, I don't. The FBI have already been here, Rick. They know everything. You need to turn yourself in and see if you can cut a –"

"That's what I'm trying to do, you dumb bitch. But I can't do it without the money."

"Yes, you can. I know an agent. The one who brought – the one who came here to talk to me. He can help—"

"I want that money."

"Rick, that money is the least of your worries. The FBI doesn't want it. It's simply a trail that leads back to that mobster. What they want is to put him behind bars."

"And what I want is that money so that after I turn state's evidence against Moretti I can get away."

"But the FBI can help you with that. They have witness protection and—"

Her head whipped to one side from the slap he gave her, before he slammed her into the side of the car. She righted herself, staring at him in shock. He pressed in close and his breath was foul in her face. "You listen to me. You're going to give me that money. Moretti already probably has men headed here since that story came out about you screwing that old cowboy actor. How long do you think it's going to be before they find you?

"And let me assure you that they won't think twice about killing you, Analise."

"What purpose would that serve? I don't have the money. It's in David's—" Sudden realization had her stopping in mid-sentence. "They'll kill me and David and then the trust will go to you. You don't want the money to escape, you want to try and buy your life back."

"I'll do whatever it takes to get Moretti off my ass. If it means giving him what you took, then so be it. I'll do it and he'll think I'm loyal. Then I can turn on him. With what I have I can leave the country. But I need that money to make my plan work, so you're going to give it to me. One way or the other.

"Please, for our son's sake, take the easy way."

Analise couldn't believe the man standing in front of her was someone she'd shared more than twenty years of her life with. He spoke of ending her and their son's life with no more regard than swatting an annoying fly.

"You'd let them kill me, Rick? And our son? Just like that?"

"Don't get all high and mighty with me. You're the one fucking some washed- out actor in this backwater hell-hole."

Analise opened her mouth, ready to deliver a scathing diatribe on his audacity but then changed her mind. It was clear that Rick had lost whatever feelings he'd once had for her and their son. All he cared about was saving his own ass and escaping.

"I can't just give you the money, Rick. It's in a trust. I'd have to get my attorney involved and it's Saturday. He won't be in his office until Monday morning."

"Fine, then on Monday that's just what you'll do."

"Fine. I'll do that. Do you have a phone? I'll call you when—"

She never got to finish the sentence. The last thing she saw was his fist coming at her face.

*****

Riley had not taken two steps into the bar before Cody was yelling at him from across the room. "Where's Annie?"

"With you."

"She's not with me. I waited twenty minutes and called her a dozen times."

Riley felt like his heart had just jumped up in his throat. He pulled out his phone and called Analise. It went straight to voice mail. "Call me, Annie." He ended the call and texted her.

Where are you?

When there was no immediate response, he called David. "Hey, David. Is your mom with you?"

"I thought she was with you."

"Have you talked to her in the last hour or so?"

"No. Why? Is something wrong?"

"I don't know. Why don't you head over to the bar."

"On my way."

Riley ended the call to find the entire Sweet family, standing at the bar watching him. "Well?" Cody asked from behind the bar.

"He hasn't seen or talked to her."

"Well when's the last time you saw her?" Billy asked.

"When she left to go meet Cody and come here."

"Where were you?" Cody asked.

"Standing in front of the hardware store."

"That's two blocks from the bakery," Hannah commented.

Riley turned on his heel but stopped at a yell from Cody. " Where're you going?" She ran from behind the bar to him.

"To look. Call Tom. I think he's on duty."

"You think something's happened to her, don't you? Like that guy who hit your truck? What's going on, Riley?"

"I don't have time to explain now. I need to find her, Cody."

"We'll all look."

"You have things to do. I can't ask—"

Cody shook her head. "We don't open 'till six. That gives us an hour. With all of us we can cover the town faster."

"We're on it, Riley." Billy announced.

"Thank you." Riley gave the family a nod. "Call me if you find her."

"We will." Cody gave his arm a squeeze. "We'll find her."

Riley headed out to his truck. Just as he reached it, Bobby drove up. David jumped out of the passenger's side. "What's going on?"

"We need to find your mother."

"Where do we look?"

"Start with town. Call if you find her."

"You too." David ran back to Bobby's truck and climbed in. By the time Riley had started his truck, Bobby's was disappearing down the road.

His insides were in a knot. Something had happened. Analise would not have left Cody in the lurch. She'd have called if she were not going to show. Something had prevented that. But what?

That's the question that scared him.

*****

Analise woke and for a moment was disoriented. Until it hit her what had happened. She was in the backseat of a car. A car that wasn't moving. There was no one in the driver's seat. She pushed herself up to look outside.

The car was parked on the side of a dirt road. When she looked through the rear window she could see they were not far off a paved road. It had to be the road to someone's house. There was a mailbox at the end of the dirt road where it intersected the pavement.

She scanned her surroundings and jumped when she spotted Rodrick. He was behind a tree, pulling down his pants. Now there was a sight she never expected to see. It was also the chance she needed. As quietly as possible she crawled into the front, slid the key out of the ignition and eased out of the driver's side door. She didn't bother to close it, she just took off running.

A yell from behind her let her know that Rodrick had spotted her. She ran faster, headed for the main road. She was almost there when she heard him yelling her name. Analise didn't bother to look behind her. She had a good head start and nothing was going to stop her from reaching the main road and flagging down help, or running all the way back to town if she had to.

She reached the main road and paused to look one way and then the other. The handwritten name on the mailbox read Miller. That gave her no real clue, where she was, but she had to choose a direction. On impulse she turned to the right. She tossed the car key as far as she could off the side of the road and reached for her back pocket. Yes! Her phone was still there. Running as fast as she could made digging her phone out of her pocket a bit difficult but she managed.

She dialed 911, pressed send and the speaker button. A few seconds later the call went through. "Cotton Creek Police Department."

"This is Analise Becke. I was abducted and managed to get away from my captor, but I'm running down a road with him chasing me and I don't know where I am. I was on a dirt road and there was a mailbox at the end that read Miller. I turned right onto a paved road."

"Slow down, Miss. You're where?"

"I don't know where. Can't you ping my phone or something?"

"Stay on the line."

Analise dared to look behind her. She didn't see anything. Maybe he had given up. Relief had her slowing her pace.

"Mrs. Becke?" A man's voice came on the line. "This is Deputy Greene. Can you tell me where you are?"

"No. A paved road. Two lanes. That's all I know. I just left a road with a mailbox with the name Miller on it."

"Are there any other houses or structures?"

Analise scanned both sides of the road. There was a mailbox ahead. "There's a mail box up ahead. I'll be there in a minute. Just hold on."

She increased her pace and was winded by the time she reached the next mailbox. Chipped paint on its side spelled the word Hawkins. "It says Hawkins."

"Allen Hawkin's place." She heard him say before he addressed her. "Ms. Becke I want you to head for the Hawkins' house. We're going to call and if anyone is there we'll tell them to expect you. If they're home, go inside and wait for me. If they are not home, I want you to find a place you can hide around the house. A place where you can see if anyone drives up. Do you understand?"

"Yes."

"Okay, do you need dispatch to stay on the line here with you?"

"No. No, I want to talk to Riley."

"I'm going to call him now. He and the Sweets are out looking for you. I'll have him call."

"Okay. Okay. Thanks."

"Now do just as I told you. Do you understand?""

"Yes. If the Hawkins are home go inside and wait for you. If they're not home, find a place to hide so I can see if anyone drives up. You'll have Riley call me."

"Yes. Good. We'll be there as fast as we can, Ms. Becke."

"Thank you."

She was just ending the call when the house came into sight. There were no cars parked around it. She ran to the front door and knocked. When there was no answer, she hopped off the front porch and ran around to the back. No one answered her knock at the back door either.

She looked in the window beside the door. The house was dark. A noise made her jump and she hurried off the porch and continued around the back of the house. There was a small shed in the rear of the yard. Maybe she should hide there.

Once behind the shed she paced and watched her phone, willing Riley to call. Five minutes turned into ten and stretched to twelve when it dawned on her that she couldn't see or hear anyone coming to the house from where she was hiding. What if Rodrick found her?

Analise made her way back toward the front of the house. There was a big bush at the corner of the house. If she stood behind it she could see the driveway and maybe not be noticed. She worked her way behind the bush to the house and was just a foot from it when sudden fear had her heart slamming in her chest.

Even though she'd never heard one before, something primal in her activated at the sound of the rattle. She froze, looked down and almost screamed. There, not two feet away, curled up beneath the bush was a rattlesnake. One very pissed off rattlesnake from the looks of it. It's body was primed to attack, that tail shaking a hundred miles an hour and its body drawn back in preparation to launch.

She'd researched rattlesnakes once for a scene in a book but at the moment couldn't recall one single fact that would minimize the terror coursing through her. Analise tried to slow her breathing, keeping her eye on the snake. *Just be calm. Be calm.*

That was easier said than done, but she could be still. Hell, she was too scared to move anyway. It seemed like she'd been standing there for an hour when the rattle stopped. A few seconds later, the snake's body uncoiled a bit and slid to one side.

Yes, please go away. Analise wouldn't let herself move a muscle. If the snake would just move on she'd find another hiding place.

The snake moved toward the house, its body propelling it sideways while its eyes continued to regard her. Just as the head turned away from her and she started to exhale fully, the phone in her hand rang.

Analise screamed and jumped about two feet to one side at the same moment the snake coiled and then struck out. She didn't realize she'd pressed the answer button on the face of the phone. She was too busy screaming and jumping. The snake had missed her but was preparing to strike again.

In the next few seconds, confusion had her freezing. A loud report split the silence at almost the same time the snake exploded into bits of blood and gore, splattering her legs. Just as the scream ripped from her throat, someone grabbed her from behind.

Analise screamed and thrashed, beating at the hand that gripped her. "Annie! It's me. Stop!"

Recognition stole her strength and she sagged. When she turned, she looked up into Riley's face. "You okay, honey?"

She nodded, unable to find her voice.

"You're hurt."

Again she nodded.

"Let's get you to the doctor."

That's when she found her voice. "No. No. Where are the police?"

"Right behind me." Riley looked toward the drive. "Well a minute or so. What happened, Annie?"

"Rodrick. My husband. He's here. He –he knocked me out and I woke up in the back of a car. He was – he was taking a crap behind a tree so I took the car key and ran. He was chasing me."

"Your husband's here? In Cotton Creek? Why?"

"He wants the money I took. The money I put in trust for David. He's going to tell the FBI he'll testify against that mobster then take the money and run."

"We need to call Kade."

"The police need to go find him. He can't go far. Unless he found the key. No. No, I threw it away when I was running down the road."

"There's Tom." Riley looked toward the driveway.

They waited as the Deputy stopped and got out of the car. Analise told him what had happened and he got on his car radio and called it in then got out of the car again. "Riley, you want to take Ms. Becke back to town? I'll need a statement from her, but we can do that in the morning. I think you should get doc to take a look at her."

"I will. And I'll bring her down to the station in the morning."

"I'll find your – the man who did this, Ms. Becke."

"Thank you."

"Yes ma'am. Riley."

Riley nodded to Tom, then put his arm around Analise. "Let's get you over to Doc's, okay?"

"No. Please, I'm okay. I need to find David. I need to know he's okay."

"But—"

"I'm fine, Riley and I need to see my son."

"Okay. Okay. Let's go."

They got into Riley's truck. He stowed his shotgun behind the seat, climbed in and headed for town. All the way there Analise kept thinking about what Rodrick had said.

I'll do whatever it takes to get Moretti off my ass. If it means giving him what you took, then so be it. I'll do it and he'll think I'm loyal. Then I can turn on him. With what I

239

have I can leave the country. But I need that money to make my plan work, so you're going to give it to me. One way or the other

She had no doubt that he meant it which meant her son was in danger. She had to get to him, make sure he was safe. She wouldn't let Rodrick hurt him. She just had to figure out how to prevent that and how to keep her and David safe in case Rodrick was right and Moretti had people coming after them.

*****

Rodrick climbed into the passenger seat of the truck. "I appreciate the ride."

"Glad I could help. Damn odd place to find a hitchhiker. Didn't catch your name. I'm Tyler Austin."

"Rod Edwards."

"Nice to meet you Rod. What brings you to Cotton Creek?"

"Heard there was work here."

Tyler cut his eyes at Rodrick. "I'm afraid someone was pulling your leg, partner. Aside from the Pursell Ranch, I don't know anyone who's been hiring and the way I hear it Pursell is full up now."

"I guess I was told wrong."

"So where you headed?"

"To town. Is there a bus station?"

"Not really. Bus does come as far as Franklin, the county seat, but that's a good sixty miles east of here."

"Well, maybe I can catch a ride with someone. Do truckers come through here much?."

"Some.

Rodrick turned to look out of the side window, his brain in a whirl. With no car, his mobility was limited. From what he'd seen there was not a single hotel in town. He'd slept in his car the two nights he'd been there and now even that was denied him.

"So, you have a ranch?" He asked Tyler.

"Yep."

"You need any help?"

"Sorry, no, we're full up. But you know, I think I did hear something about Frank Odel who owns the feed store in town possibly looking for part-time help. I would drop you by his place but it'll be closed. Whole town is involved in homecoming this weekend.

"Thanks. I appreciate that. Maybe I can talk to him on Monday."

"Maybe so."

There was no other conversation the rest of the way to town. When they reached the edge of town, Tyler pulled over to the side of the road and stopped. "Gonna drop you here, buddy. I'm headed over to Billy's bar. They have some fine barbecue if you're interested."

"I may wander over later. Thank you again."

"Sure thing. Good luck to you."

Rodrick nodded and got out of the truck. The mention of food reminded him of two things. He hadn't eaten since yesterday and also he needed to find a bathroom. Whatever was in that Mexican food he ate last night had wrecked his digestive system.

He looked both ways up and down the street and headed into town. There had to be a place open with a bathroom. Maybe that bakery. He picked up his pace and spotted the bakery a block down and across the street.

Rodrick trotted across the road and between two cars parked parallel alongside the curb. Just as he neared the entrance of the bakery, his arm was grabbed.

"Hello Rick."

Rodrick's heart sank and his gut clenched. He knew that voice. Jimmy DeLuca was one of Giancarlo's men. He turned to face Jimmy and saw the man sitting in the backseat of the black sedan parked at the curb.

That sight did more than make his gut clench. It released his sphincter.

*****

"Just a few bruises. Nose isn't broken. You'll be fine." Doc Turner announced.

"So, there's no reason I can't go help Cody like I said I would." Analise cut her eyes at Riley as she spoke.

"None that I can see."

"Thank you. What do I owe you, Doctor Turner?"

"I'll send you a bill."

"Send it to my place." Riley said.

"Will do. Now, I think I'm going to head to Billy's as well. Missus should be there."

"Then let us get out of your hair." Riley held out his hand to Analise and when she took it, pulled her to her feet. "Thanks, Doc."

"You bet."

Riley and Analise headed out to his truck. She reached for the door handle but he stopped her turned her around and backed her up against the door. "You really think you're up to working tonight?"

"Well what would you have me do, Riley? Go sit at your house and chew my nails?"

"No, but—but your husband abducted you, Annie. And he might try again."

"At Billy's? Oh, David's there, right?"

"Yes. Cody's keeping an eye on him as well as the rest of the family. Bobby's there with him. He's safe."

"And I will be too. Rodrick's not going to try anything in a bar full of people."

Riley regarded her for a few minutes. "I'm having a hard time buying this."

"Buying what?"

"That you're okay – that what happened didn't have an effect on you."

"I didn't say that. It did. But I can't go crawl in a hole and hide. You heard Kade when we called him. He said he'd have someone here before the night was over. And the Cotton Creek police are on the alert. Even if Rick did try something he'd fail."

"I won't let him get you again, Annie. I promise you that."

"And I'm trusting you one hundred percent. Which is why we should go to Billy's and enjoy the evening. Besides, you're singing tonight and I'm hoping to hear a love song."

"A love song?"

243

"It's every girl's dream, Riley." She grabbed his shirt to tug him close. "A handsome cowboy crooner on stage singing about love. His gaze seeking you out and making you feel like you're the only girl in the room."

"The only one that matters, honey."

"See? I'm already getting dreamy."

Riley smiled. "You continue to surprise me, Wildcat."

She smiled up at him. "And you continue to be my hero. I love you…" Sudden fears had her changing directions in the conversation. "Riley, is this all too soon, too fast? I know what I feel about you. Heck, I was fantasizing about you before I ever heard your voice, and I guess I sort of fell in love with you – with the man you are before I even met you. But still, is it real? Can someone fall this hard, this fast?"

"Apparently so, since I'm right there with you."

"So…so do you think it's wrong? Me loving you, living with you, when I'm not even divorced?

Riley's eyes searched hers for a long time before he spoke. "You once said that you and your husband hadn't lived like man and wife for over five years."

"Yes, that's true."

"So do you really think that was being married? Just living in the same house?"

"But legally—"

"Annie, honey, I've been there – three times and can tell you from experience that a piece of paper isn't what makes a marriage or a relationship. It's what's in here." He put his hand to his heart. "Love is what makes it a marriage, not the paper."

"I so love you."

"That was pretty good, wasn't it?"

He laughed when she pinched his side. "You're bad, Riley Morgan. Downright bad."

"Not as bad as I will be later." He wagged his eyebrows at her.

"Promises, promises." She said and laughed. "Okay, let's go hot stuff. Cody will be standing on her head."

"Nothing new there." He reached around her to open the truck door.

When she climbed in he stepped up close to kiss her. "I love you, Annie."

Hearing those words filled her with hope. Hope that all this mess with Rodrick could be settled and she could stay here, with Riley and hear those words every day. For the rest of her life.

Chapter Eighteen

"Oops! Sorry." Analise smiled at the heavyset cowboy as she bumped into him with a tray of empty glasses.

"No problem, little lady."

She took the glasses to the dirty glass bin behind the bar and shouted out an order to Cody. "Two Jacks and coke and three drafts."

"Pull the drafts. Jack and cokes in two shakes."

Just as Analise was loading up the tray, her replacement, Beverly Mills, a part-time girl in her mid-twenties, showed up. "Hey! I'll take that for you. Where's it go?"

"Over there on the left, the four top that has five at it. Three ladies and two men."

"On it."

Analise grabbed a glass to dispense herself a soft drink, but before she could fill it, Cody snatched it out of her hand. "Replacements are here and it's time to kick back, girlfriend."

"And what do you recommend?" Analise shouted to be heard over the crowd.

Cody held up two shot glasses. "Tequila, baby. Top shelf."

"No lime or salt?."

"That's for pussies. Bottoms up."

Analise tossed back the tequila shot and sucked in a breath. "Well, *that* hit the spot. Now what?"

Cody cocked her head to one side as Riley stepped up to the microphone on the stage. "Folks, you reckon it's time?"

A chorus of cheers and hoots went up and Riley laughed. "All righty then. Let's hear it for Billy Sweet's Honkytonk Angels."

The band started up a popular song and Cody turned to Analise. "Now we dance. You line dance, right?"

"Uh, a little. Very little."

"That's okay, you'll catch on. Hannah!"

"What?" Hannah yelled from the other end of the bar where she was stuffing money into the cash register.

"Time for our honky tonk routine, little sister."

Hannah threw back her head and let out a rebel yell that shocked Analise. A moment later, she sashayed to where Analise and Cody stood, took Analise by the hand and led her to the small step-stool at the corner of the bar.

"Follow me."

"Honky tonk routine?" Analise looked back at Cody in shock as Hannah stepped up on top of the bar. "Yep. Now get going, girl." Cody said and grinned.

"Well, when in Rome..." Analise climbed up on the bar and a moment later so did Cody.

"Move down a bit and just do what we do." Cody yelled.

That's just what Analise did and in less than a minute she had it. The yells and hoots from the crowd were deafening. She laughed, clapped and danced, singing at the top of her lungs.

The song was on its last chorus and everyone in the bar was singing, and either dancing or cheering from their seats. In the few seconds that followed a series of events had Analise's mind in a state of complete confusion and fear.

Gunfire erupted, three shots. Right after that two things happened almost simultaneously. First there was the sound of guns cocking, unarmed people hitting the floor while at least fifty armed men drew beads on the three suited men who now stood out in the crowd like sore thumbs. Before all of that could fully register in Analise's mind, two sounds intruded. A long wailing siren and what sounded like the noise of an approaching train.

"Twister!" Someone shouted.

That one word had chaos ensuing. People on the floor were scrambling to their feet, heedless of the armed assailants, yelling and screaming. Cody yelled at Analise. "The back office. Now!"

Analise had no clue what that meant, but the way Cody and Hannah were scrambling off the bar and headed toward the back office scared her. The roar of wind increased and people were scurrying for cover, crowding around and behind the bar, rushing toward the kitchen and bathrooms.

Her gaze swept toward the stage. It was empty. Where was Riley? And where was David? As she searched the crowd, a shock had her entire body jumping. Rodrick was there. With a beautiful young woman and an older man in an expensive suit.

She couldn't quite comprehend what was going on and the ability to consider it was cut short when someone grabbed her arm and yanked her down from the bar. Riley.

"Get to the office." He shouted. "Cellar door is there."

"I have to find David!"

"I told him to go to the office. Now move!"

Analise took two steps and then jumped as gunfire erupted and the wood around her feet exploded in splinters and chunks. A dozen shots followed accompanied by screams. Riley threw her to the floor and dove on top of her.

She squirmed to be able to see. Three of the assailants were on the floor and the well-dressed man now had one arm around the throat of a hostage. David. The man had a gun pointed at his head. "Anyone moves and the boy dies." The man shouted.

"No!" Analise squirmed and fought to get Riley off her. "No!"

"You!" The man shouted and looked at the young woman standing beside Rodrick. "That's her."

The woman's arm rose. In her hand was a gun. It was pointed directly at Analise. "Kill the bitch." The man ordered.

Analise saw the smile on the woman's face and suddenly everything went into slow motion as she waited for death. She saw Rodrick grab the woman. They wrestled for the gun and he managed to get it away from her and shove her. She tripped and went down.

Rodrick pointed the gun at the well-dressed man. "Let him go, Moretti."

"It's him or your wife." Moretti shouted back. "Kill her or I put a bullet through his head."

Strength she didn't know she possessed filled her and Analise wiggled free of Riley and scrambled to her feet. "Go ahead, Rick. Shoot me, but let David go. You can't let him kill our son. Please."

"Mom, no!" David shouted at the same moment Riley stepped in front of her.

"Riley!" She tried to get around him, but he prevented her, shouting at Moretti. "You've got at least a dozen guns on you right now. Either one of you fires and you're dead. You hear me?"

Analise didn't see how anyone could. She could barely hear him. The roar of the wind was too loud. Moretti must have heard at least part of it, because he started backing towards the door, keeping his arm locked around David's neck and the gun pointed at his head.

Rodrick grabbed the young woman and jammed his gun to her head. "Shoot him and she dies!"

Analise screamed but the scream was lost. Shrieks from the structure preceded a great tearing sound just before a section of the roof above the stage was ripped away. The end section of the bar that housed the stage suddenly was sucked away into what looked like a nightmare of swirling black air and the entire roof sagged in toward the opening.

Tables and chairs, bottles and glasses were sucked into the maelstrom, becoming projectiles that buffeted the remaining walls and the people lying on the floor, hanging onto anything they could to try and prevent being sucked into the twister.

Riley wrapped one arm around Analise and the other around the corner post of the bar. She could feel the force pulling at her and she clung to him with all her strength. "David!"

David couldn't hear her. He and Moretti were being pulled closer to the maelstrom. Moretti lost his grip and Analise screamed as David was literally lifted up off the floor.

What happened next was beyond anything she could have imagined. Joe was suddenly there. He wrapped his arms around David and suddenly David was on his feet again, standing in the middle of a hell of debris that jetted around him.

Moretti managed to raise his arm and point his gun at David. Analise couldn't even scream she was so terrified. She felt like her heart was going to explode in her chest. Rodrick was clinging to a post, his body being pulled away from it. When he let go with one arm and fired at Moretti, she gasped. Moretti fell, clutching his chest and the woman with Rodrick turned on him, hands drawn into claws.

Rodrick looked at David. "I'm sorry."

In the next instant, he grabbed the woman and released his hold on the post. In horror, Analise watched as both of them were pulled out into the churning nightmare. No more than a few seconds later, the twister roared away, leaving an eerie silence in its wake.

Analise sagged in Riley's arm, her eyes glued to David, who stood in the middle of the destruction, looking dazed, held in Joe's arms. David smiled and her and she breathed a sigh of relief before turning to Riley.

"We made it."

"Yeah, Wildcat, we –"

A deafening groan had her whirling around and looking up. The last thing she remembered was hearing Riley say "oh shit", the feel of his arms tightening around her and Joe throwing his arms out wide.

Then the roof came down.

Chapter Nineteen

Analise winced as she pushed herself out of the chair at the table. When the roof at Billy's Bar collapsed, she and many others had miraculously survived. She had a couple of fractured ribs, but they were on the mend. David had suffered no injuries and Riley had escaped with only four stitches in his head.

The emergency teams from the fire department of the nearest two counties were called in and everyone claimed it was a miracle that there were so few injuries and no fatalities. Analise knew better. She'd seen Joe protect David and she'd seen him throw his arms out protectively. She had no doubt who had saved them.

Riley got up and offered his hand. "You okay, honey?"

"Yeah. I'm fine. Just wanted to finish all this up before we head in to see Billy's bar. Cody said the family would meet us there. The repairs on their house are almost done so they'll be moving out of the ranch house next week and back to town."

"Not a minute too soon for Cody, I imagine."

Analise chuckled. "Well, the place is as clean as a whistle with Stella and Hannah there, but having everyone around is driving her a little nuts. She likes the quiet."

"I get that."

"Are we too much for you, Riley?" Worries rose fast. "David and me, I mean."

"Never. You're my family."

"Are we?"

"You know you are, Wildcat." He pulled her into his arms and hers wound around his waist.

"He's leaving at the end of the week. To go back to school."

"Yeah, I know. I'm gonna miss him."

"Me too. But – but I know it's right for him and I think now…" She let the rest of the words go unsaid.

David now knew that despite his father not showing interest and being aloof, he had actually loved David. He'd killed to protect David. Analise was still amazed by the fact. She'd never imagined Rodrick as the self-sacrificing type of man. But in the end, he had been and to her that meant he'd found redemption.

"You sure you're okay, Annie?"

"Yes. I am. I just – I just think about it. Rick and that woman Gina. That was a horrible death. I hope – I hope he didn't suffer."

"Coroner said they both died on impact."

She nodded. "And thank god, the police found that thumb drive in Moretti's pocket, the one he apparently took from Rick. It cleared his name and that's important for David. He doesn't have to go through life being stained by the brush of corruption."

"Amen to that. I guess by now, the rest of the family is well on their way to prison."

"According to Kade, it won't be long. The government's case against them is iron- clad. And when I spoke to him earlier, he said that the Moretti family's syndicate was done as well. Rick might have made some horrible mistakes, but in the end he came through, didn't he? He saved David and brought down that whole operation."

"Yeah. He did. And I know that gives you comfort."

"It does. Now I – I can go on with my life with a clear conscience. I don't have to hate him and I don't have to look over my shoulder."

"The way I hear it, you and David have some surprises in store for a few folks."

She smiled up at him. "We do and it's all thanks to you."

"Me?"

"Yes. After everything was settled with all that – that mess, David came to you, remember?"

"I remember having a talk – about what he wanted to do with his life and about life in general."

"A lot of people had told him things about you, Riley. About the man you are and how you help others. It made a big impact on him. One I think you're going to be really proud of."

"So you're not going to tell me either?"

"Nope. David and I made a deal. You'll find out when we go over to the bar."

"Well I'm ready when you are."

"Okay." She turned and grabbed a folder off the table. "David is meeting us there. Bobby's going to drive him over.

"Then let's do it."

After a quick kiss, they headed out. All the way into town Analise thought about what had happened since she left New York. Some of it had been horrible and some a true blessing. And some of it was verging on the edge of miraculous.

She looked over at Riley behind the wheel. "Kade said you had a conversation with him about Joe."

Riley shook his head and cut a look at her. "I'm still on the fence on that one, honey. I mean I saw the man, the way he protected David and I still don't know why no one else but us saw him. Kade said – well you know. But I have a hard time wrapping my mind around it."

"There are more things in heaven and earth, Horatio."

"Than are dreamt of in your philosophy." He finished and grinned. "Well, who knows what's possible right? I mean look at us. Online friends who fell in love."

Analise chuckled. "Yeah, never saw that coming."

"But I'm glad it did." He reached over and took her hand. They finished the rest of the drive in silence. When they arrived at the bar, the Sweet family was there, all gathered around the tailgate of Billy's truck, along with David and Bobby.

Analise and Riley climbed out of his truck and walked over to the family. She looked at what was left of the bar. "Every time I see it I'm amazed that no one was killed."

"We were durn lucky, that's for sure." Billy said. "Dave says you have something you want to tell us."

"Yes." Analise looked at David. "After all that mess was settled with the FBI and my husband's estate, David and I made some decisions about our life."

She looked at Riley. "I'm staying here in Cotton Creek. I'd like to call this home." She then looked back at the Sweet family. "The government gave us all the money Rick took. We – we don't feel right about keeping it so we came up with a plan. David? Why don't you tell them?"

He grinned and walked over between her and Riley, draping an arm around each of them. "First, we're setting up a foundation for the people of Cotton Creek. I've been talking a lot to Riley and I know a lot can happen that can really hurt folks financially around here. A bad season of crops or loss of livestock can mean the difference in survival and losing all you've worked for.

"We think people like those here in Cotton Creek deserve some help when those times hit. So, we've set up a foundation. Families with hardships can apply for financial assistance. My mom will run it and we'll do all we can to help people. We'll start the foundation with sixty million dollars."

Stella clapped her hands to her mouth as tears erupted from her eyes. "Oh my lord. What a sweet—" Sobs made the rest of what she said unintelligible.

"I don't even have the words to say how kind and generous that is of you." Billy filled in the gap. "But I know folks will sure appreciate it."

"We just want to help." David said. "Make a difference."

"And what about you?" Hannah asked. "You still have to finish school. You'll need money to pay—"

"That's covered." He interrupted and gave Analise a smile. "Mom's handling that. Just like the second part of what we wanted to tell you. It was her idea and I support it a hundred percent. Mom?"

Analise smiled at him. "We've been talking to people around town and it looks like the damage from the tornado totals up to nearly four million dollars when you include the

257

damages that will have to be paid by the town. So, we're going to fund all of the repairs and renovations.

"Including your bar."

Cody slid off the tailgate with a thump. "Are you serious?"

"Absolutely." Analise said and opened her folder. "I have the papers right here. In fact, I have a little something else. Just food for thought.

"The night of the tornado, before it hit, the band – and you" she looked at Cody. "Put an idea in my head. I didn't think much about it until last week when Billy said he was giving you and Hannah the bar, so that when it was rebuilt it could be your place, just like you wanted."

"Anyway, that night, Riley said "I believe it's time for Billy Sweet's Honky Tonk Angels. And then Cody said it was time for the honky tonk angel routine." Her gaze moved to Stella. "Your mom told me that you've been doing that since you were little girls. That your dad has often referred to you as his honky tonk angels."

"It's true." Cody said and reached over to give her dad's arm a squeeze.

"So, it got me to thinking." Analise said and turned the paper so they could see what was on it. "Maybe you might want to consider this for your place. It kind of combines the old and the new. Keeps what made this place a success and adds your own touch."

Cody took one look and grinned. She looked over at Hannah and Hannah burst out with a "hell yeah!"

Analise grinned. "You like it? Really?"

"Hell yes!" Cody ran over and threw her arms around David, Analise and Riley, encompassing them all in a group hug. "Damn, ya'll, how the hell can we ever thank you for this?"

"You already did." Analise said. "You took us in, made us feel like friends and then like family. You are family to us and one thing we learned from this man here—" She looked up at Riley. "Is that family takes care of their own."

Riley smiled down at her. "You done good, Wildcat. Real good."

"Yeah?"

"Yeah."

"Hell yeah." Cody added and grinned.

Analise hugged David and Riley, her arms around their waists pulling them closer. "Then I guess we're done here."

"Not quite." Riley said.

Everyone looked at him and he looked at David. "As the man of the family, I'd like to ask your permission to marry your mother."

David grinned from ear-to-ear. "That's a big hell yes."

"Thank you, Dave. I promise I'll always treat her right and love her till my last breath."

"I know you will, Riley. And I'm gonna be real proud to call you my step-father. If you don't mind, that is."

"Son, there's nothing I would like better."

Analise watched the two people she loved most in the word hug and tears streamed down her face. This was a moment she'd never dreamed of, one that exceeded all her hopes. When they parted, Riley looked at her. "So, Wildcat, what do you say? Will you be my love and let me be yours as along as there's life in us?."

"You had me at hello, cowboy."

He burst out laughing. "As I recall, you fainted dead away."

Analise and everyone else laughed along with him. She threw her arms around Riley and the paper in her hand fluttered to the ground. It was a new day for a lot of people in Cotton Creek. New beginnings, new hopes and new dreams. And for her, it was the moment she'd dreamed of since she was a child.

She finally had it. She was home. Really home. The place that love lived.

Note for Readers

The characters Kade Lawson, Cia Whitehorse and Joe
appear in the box set "Rangers" which is available on
Amazon Kindle and free in Kindle Unlimited. Below is an
excerpt from Kade's tale.

Blurb:

Book 2 of Rangers: Silver Star Seductions

When Cia Whitehorse walks into Kade Lawson's office and
announces she's been assigned to help with a serial killer
investigation, he's damn sure he's never met a federal agent
as sexy.

Cia takes one look at Kade and makes up her mind that
she's going to have him in her bed. She might not be
interested in love, but sex is definitely right up her alley and
Kade looks like the kind of man who can give her just what
she wants.

Kade is more than willing to deliver what Cia needs. She
gets to him. Tough and sexy, with an unspoken promise in
her look that says she'll rock his world. But that look is
covering something. And Kade's a sucker for a mystery.

The problem is, solving the mystery of Cia Whitehorse
comes with a price.

Excerpt:

Kade had just finished going over the reports when one of the local detectives tapped on the doorframe. "Feds are here."

It was lucky the guy looked behind him at that moment or he would have seen the frown that creased Kade's forehead. As he had stated more than once since they'd received notice that the Bureau was sending an agent, with the Texas Rangers on the case, there was no need for feds. But since this case looked to be connected to a serial killer known as the Carver, the FBI was going to want to mark the territory as their own. As much as no one wanted to admit it, in times like these, despite the common goal, various organizations still went through pissing contests to see who was top dog.

Kade turned away from the computer screen and stood. A short woman with dark hair pulled back from her face in a long braid entered the room. She was dressed in faded, low-slung jeans, a tight black t-shirt with words in white printed across her breasts that read "Yet despite the look on my face, you're still talking," obviously old motorcycle boots, and an equally worn short leather jacket. Surely, this wasn't the federal agent?

"Can I help you?" Kade figured she had to have wandered into the wrong place.

"I'm looking for Officer Lawson."

"You've found him. How can I help you, Miss…?"

"Agent Whitehorse. Cia Whitehorse." She pulled her identification from her jacket.

He gave the identification a look as he rose. "Nice to meet you, Agent Whitehorse." He came around the desk and extended his hand.

"Cia." Her grip was firm and her gaze steady as she took his hand. Kade held on a moment longer than necessary, his eyes locked to hers. There was a lot you could figure out about a person by their eyes.

Like this one. Her gaze never wavered, her eyes never blinked. It was the stare of a predator and that of a person in hiding. There was defiance in her eyes, which probably explained the unconventional dress. Either she was out to make her mark by being one tough bitch, and daring the world to stand against her, or she was someone running from herself and using her job as a place to hide from her own demons.

He wasn't sure which, but either way, when he added those observations to the sexual energy pouring off her, she spelled one thing. Trouble.

"You gonna let go and get down to it, or ask me to go steady?" The look in her eyes changed with the question. It was a clear message that he was crossing a line, but one delivered in a slightly offhand sexual manner.

He smiled and released her hand, watching the slow smile on her face. Funny, but it never reached her eyes. Another clue. This was definitely a woman with secrets. Damn bad thing for him because he was a total sucker for mysteries.

But right now, there were more important matters on the table. "We've got you set up over there." He gestured to the desk adjacent to the one he'd been assigned. "Everything on the case has been loaded onto the computer. I'll get you set up and after you've had time to—"

"I've already been over all of it on the way here. I'd like to see the scene and the body."

"Where first?"

"The scene."

He gestured toward the door. "After you."

She pivoted and led the way. Kade followed, trying not to notice the enticing sway of her ass in her jeans. Of all the luck. He got assigned lead in one of the biggest cases of his career and was saddled to temptation in denim.

Well, he'd just have to resist temptation. How hard could it be? It wasn't as if she was likely to jump his bones. Although, that thought did bring a few lascivious thoughts to mind that were likely to return in detail when he was alone in bed tonight.

About the Author

You can find all of Ciana's books on her
Amazon author page

Books by Ciana Stone

Hot in the Saddle

Untamed: A Three Book Box Set

The Whisperers: Simply Irresistible – A Three Book Box
Set

Holdin' On for a Hero: A three book set

Tales of Betrayal, passion, danger and love

Hunger: The V'Kar Series – A three book set

The Sins of Love – Renegades Book 1

Coming of Age

On My Knees – The Seven Book 1

Ruffle My Feathers – The Seven Book 2

With a Little Help From My Friends

Wrath: Voodoo's Angel

The Seven: A Taste for Jazz

Made in the USA
Monee, IL
21 April 2021